Get in, cause chaos, locate and secure the target

Hardly a detailed battle plan, but it would suffice. Bolan crouched and watched intently, not flinching as the blast went off forty-five degrees to his right. His attention was focused entirely on the encampment.

The guards broke formation and began to rush toward the explosion. He could see the two Russian bosses yelling and trying to establish some kind of order.

Bolan couldn't let that happen. He triggered another explosion a little less than 180 degrees opposite.

The complete force congregated at the sound of the second blast. Sighting, he tapped off four short bursts and two men dropped, one with his face blown away and the other losing half the side of his head.

Having given away his own position and attracted return fire, he needed to move. He triggered an explosion only fifty yards from him to throw up a cloud cover, then Bolan crawled at double speed in the opposite direction.

As he circled, he wondered how he would progress from here. He could try to pick them off. But the Executioner was running short of charges…and the Russians would soon catch on. If they hadn't already.

MACK BOLAN ®
The Executioner

The Don Pendleton's
Executioner®

COLD FUSION

A GOLD EAGLE BOOK FROM
WORLDWIDE®

TORONTO • NEW YORK • LONDON
AMSTERDAM • PARIS • SYDNEY • HAMBURG
STOCKHOLM • ATHENS • TOKYO • MILAN
MADRID • WARSAW • BUDAPEST • AUCKLAND

Recycling programs
for this product may
not exist in your area.

First edition February 2013

ISBN-13: 978-0-373-64411-7

Special thanks and acknowledgment to
Andy Boot for his contribution to this work.

COLD FUSION

Copyright © 2013 by Worldwide Library

Printed in U.S.A.

The release of atom power has changed everything except our way of thinking... the solution to this problem lies in the heart of mankind. If only I had known, I should have become a watchmaker.

—Albert Einstein

The most dangerous weapon of all is the human mind. Of this there is no doubt. Luckily I have a very sharp one of my own.

—Mack Bolan

THE
MACK BOLAN
LEGEND

Nothing less than a war could have fashioned the destiny of the man called Mack Bolan. Bolan earned the Executioner title in the jungle hell of Vietnam.

But this soldier also wore another name—Sergeant Mercy. He was so tagged because of the compassion he showed to wounded comrades-in-arms and Vietnamese civilians.

Mack Bolan's second tour of duty ended prematurely when he was given emergency leave to return home and bury his family, victims of the Mob. Then he declared a one-man war against the Mafia.

He confronted the Families head-on from coast to coast, and soon a hope of victory began to appear. But Bolan had broken society's every rule. That same society started gunning for this elusive warrior—to no avail.

So Bolan was offered amnesty to work within the system against terrorism. This time, as an employee of Uncle Sam, Bolan became Colonel John Phoenix. With a command center at Stony Man Farm in Virginia, he and his new allies—Able Team and Phoenix Force—waged relentless war on a new adversary: the KGB.

But when his one true love, April Rose, died at the hands of the Soviet terror machine, Bolan severed all ties with Establishment authority.

Now, after a lengthy lone-wolf struggle and much soul-searching, the Executioner has agreed to enter an "arm's-length" alliance with his government once more, reserving the right to pursue personal missions in his Everlasting War.

1

"It's too cold," Asif Bhayat complained as he shifted on the surface of the sand. Loose grains blew in the cold night air and got in his hair, nose and mouth. Yet the hard-packed sand beneath him made him shift uncomfortably as he shouldered the HK PSG1 that he had spent so long learning to use.

"It's always cold at night. And too hot in the day," Hussein Ali murmured. "If you don't like it, then go home and leave the fighting to those who can take it."

"I'm not complaining," Bhayat muttered.

"You always are," his companion replied.

The two men fell into an uneasy silence while Bhayat nestled the semi-automatic rifle into his shoulder and sighted through the Hensoldt ZF6x42PSG1 telescopic sight. Its illuminated reticle made the distant camp seem as clear as in the glare of the midday sun.

They were fifteen klicks to the west of Jaghbub, one of the few oases that eased the aridity of the desert. When Bhayat had first been told that he was being sent to Libya and that he would be in the desert, he hadn't bothered to look it up and learn about the area. A bit of sand and a few days between waterholes—easy.

Bhayat had been an urban boy, fired up by the talk of jihad and intent on playing his part in the holy revolution. The closest he had come to sand and heat was the occasional coastal holiday in a specially designed resort. He'd had no idea what it would really entail.

Through the sight he could see guards moving along the perimeter of the small encampment. There were two, moving clockwise and counterclockwise around the four tents. The circumference of their orbit encompassed the tents and the three vehicles. All three were jeeps, which—doing the math quickly—meant that the party was probably a dozen men in total: fifteen, sixteen at most, and that would be unlikely given the equipment they carried.

There were eight in this raid party. Bhayat and Ali as one pair, and three others who had slowly worked their way into position around the camp. It had taken most of the night. Communication was kept to a bare minimum as it was likely their enemy had the tech to intercept. Distance was also a factor—the enemy had guards, but they may also have motion detectors. Though it was unlikely that such tech would work efficiently in this environment; too much shifting in the sand could trigger reactions all night. Briefly, Bhayat smiled at the thought of their enemy having interrupted rest because of the sands and the insects that crawled within.

Regardless, this was not the time to take chances. Intel had told them that the enemy included an American—one who had been observed with the enemy and whose demeanour had demanded caution.

Bhayat flexed his finger on the trigger of the PSG1. One of the guards was in the center of the sight, a head shot that would be safe and easy.

Two problems. First, it was too soon. He could tell by the way that Ali was holding himself against the sand that the time was not right. Second, the sight was accurate to nine hundred yards. Even with no way to measure, he could tell that he was more than a thousand yards away.

Bhayat relaxed his finger and took his eye away from the sight. He turned his head and saw Ali looking directly at him.

"You're learning," the older man murmured.

"WHY NOT EGYPT?" Jared Hassim asked the American. "Why the move to here?"

Bolan grinned mirthlessly. "It's harder to hit a moving target. Especially if it moves one step ahead all the time."

"But I don't understand." The older man sighed. "They are, after all, merchants. They wish to sell. Why do they make it so hard for those who wish to buy? Surely they should set up their stall, make their sale and run with the money. They messed up first time, yes? Then why not make the second time easier? If what they are selling is so wonderful, why do they wish to make it so hard for those who will flock to them?"

The two men sat on the tarp floor of the tent. A lamp lit the interior dimly. Between them sat a small table, with Bolan's iPad dead center. The soldier swung it around so that it was right way up for Hassim.

"Take a look at that," he said simply.

The older man looked at the screen for a few seconds, then up at Bolan, shrugging. "Tell me what I am seeing. I am a simple man."

Bolan chuckled. "Simple is one thing you've never been, Jared. You forget how long I've known you. It's a good act, but I remember you at West Point."

"So I spent too long in deep cover before finally going rogue. So shoot me."

"I probably should. And maybe you have spent too long out here to see the obvious. Look at this sweep here…" Bolan indicated an area of the map of Northeast Africa that was displayed on the tablet. His finger traced a line as he spoke. "Syria, Lebanon, Israel, Jordan, Egypt, Libya. One hell of a sweep and none of it settled in recent times. When there is civil war and unrest, it gives those with an agenda plenty of room to hide. Intel told us they were in Syria, but you know what happened there. Since then, it's been about trying to play catch-up. You know they passed through Jordan, and you told me yourself they would skip over Israel and Lebanon—"

"No one wants to come under the hand of Mossad," Hassim muttered, kissing his teeth.

"Not if they have any sense," Bolan agreed. "So it was either Egypt or Libya. You had your bet, right? The former is a good land for merchants, but Libya…"

"Libya has space to hide," Hassim nodded. "Desert. A lot of it."

"Ninety percent of the country, by most estimates. All bar a few oases inhospitable—not a place to spend any amount of time, but if your buyers are ready to get in and out quickly, a good place to have an auction."

Jared raised his eyebrows. "Must be big buyers…bigger than I first thought. And so it must be a good piece of merchandise…"

"It is," Bolan affirmed simply.

THE PATROLS CROSSED again, without a word. Both men were cold and tired, and were determined to keep whatever focus they had firmly upon the darkness beyond the low-level ambient light around them.

When Bolan and Jared had determined to pitch camp for the night, they had chosen this remote section of oasis. They were on the tip of the Qattarra Depression, and far from the largest of the oases. Even given that anyone traveling—for whatever forsaken reason—through the desert would wish to stay close to the oases within the Depression, choosing this one lessened their chances of being stumbled upon by any party other than one searching for them. Anyone else was almost certain to be an enemy.

The two guards crossed for a reason. Although it meant that the rear of their patrol would be exposed for a time, it enabled them to check that each was still active without breaking radio silence. The almost flat, gently undulating sands stretched out before and behind them. The distance an enemy would need to cover made it almost impossible for any to reach the camp before they would be spotted.

The war party had kept the light from their camp to a minimum—each thick tent was lit only by a lamp that was dimmed. Any light that escaped was negligible. Despite the clear and star-spangled sky above them, the ambient light of the desert was almost zero, and beyond a short distance it was impossible for either guard to see anything with the naked eye.

As well, then, that both men wore monocular night vision headsets, using the infrared setting only. Heat at this distance would be too low to truly register. The monocles looked strange and alien as they covered the top half of the face; their lower faces were covered by kaffiyehs that kept out the worst excesses of the night cold and the sand that was carried almost as the air. Rather than the usual check pattern, these were black, woven to lend camouflage in the night. Similarly, the camo worn by the guards was dark rather than daytime light. Only their heavy desert combat boots stayed the same whatever the hour.

So dark against a background of black, both men felt that they could not be visible to any enemy by the naked eye— but who needs a naked eye?

HUSSEIN ALI'S BREATHING was slow and shallow. His body felt at rest on the unyielding sands. He would soon need all the energy and speed he could muster, and so was only too pleased to be resting—unlike his companion. He cast a side-ways glance at Asif Bhayat. The man was about a decade younger, and soft. One of the weekend warriors stirred up by rhetoric, yet ill-prepared for the realities of war. Some of them toughened up, learned what they needed. Some did not. They fell by the wayside, either casualties of action or discarded. Bhayat would probably go that way. But there would be no return home if discarded, and Ali would not be averse to settling the matter himself. He neither liked nor disliked the man who lay beside him. He saw him simply as a liability. Liabilities were costly, and Ali did not wish to pay with his own life.

He could see that the young man was itching to move. So much so that he was poised, wound tighter than a coil. Chances were that when the moment came, he would do something stupid. He was learning, but not quickly enough for war. As Ali watched, Bhayat used the Hensoldt to sight one of the guards again.

"Too far," Ali murmured.

"I know. Just keeping my eye in," Bhayat replied in an undertone.

Beneath the folds of the robe Ali had swathed around his body was the sound of a crackling. Without taking his eyes from either Bhayat or the camp in the distance, Ali extracted a battered and ancient walkie-talkie from his swaddling.

"Code Three," a thick voice said indistinctly.

"Affirmative," Ali replied carefully. The walkie-talkies were over twenty-five years old, as ancient in tech terms as the ways of the Berber, Bedouin and Tuareg who still used them. They broke down, they were unclear, and they were unwieldy. But more than any of this, they were so old that they might as well have been flags and smoke as far as the sophisticated sensors of the modern military were concerned.

Under the wire, under the radar—there were many terms to describe it. It didn't matter—it worked.

Ali grinned at his younger partner; even in the dark, Bhayat could see that the grin was not mirrored by the glittering ice of the eyes.

"Now we go…"

"So, what can they have that is so important that representatives of every government in Asia, Africa and China—not to mention a few from the Steppes and beyond as well as some of your boys who would rather remain anonymous—would scurry across Northeast Africa at their very whim? What do these men know? Some kind of chemical weapon, maybe? Warheads, perhaps, with atomic capability that have somehow disappeared from one inventory, to appear just as mysteriously on another?"

"Nothing like that," Bolan shook his head. "Not even weaponry in the conventional sense."

"Then, why would so many be so keen? You've never really explained what we're chasing. Who, yes…but not what. A cache of armaments, maybe something new to give an edge. That's usually the only thing to make these people move."

"Ordinarily," Bolan agreed. "But not this time. Not in itself. But the implications of having it—"

"Must be something worth the odd shekel or two, eh?" Hassim rubbed his fingers together in the traditional gesture. "Or bonded securities, at least."

Bolan smiled. "Guess it's time to do the big reveal. Ever hear of a thing called cold fusion?"

2

Ali moved over the sand, keeping to his belly and crawling like a sand snake. He could hear Bhayat struggling in his wake, and though he cursed, he did not look back. There was little time to waste as it was. The dark would only be cover as long as they stayed beyond the range of the night vision monocles worn by the guards. In the vast silent tract of the desert he knew that it would be impossible to mask the sound of their advance. The sand that moved through the night air did not carry with it the moaning of desert storms. He knew that the grunting young soldier would betray them before too long.

All along he had been counting in his head, measuring distance and time as he moved. He knew how long he should wait, and how far he should be able to travel.

He stopped suddenly, holding up his hand behind him to stay his companion.

"Silence," he whispered as he heard Bhayat draw breath as though to speak. "Seven hundred yards. Our range. Theirs, too."

Bhayat slithered up alongside the older man, staying silent. He understood. Raising the PSG1 to his shoulder, he settled himself in the sand and sighted. Through the Hensoldt he could see that the two guards were just coming into view at the far edges of his vision.

"Thirty seconds and we can take them both," he whispered.

"Don't be overambitious, boy." As he spoke, Ali drew an RPG-7 that he had been carrying slung across his wiry shoulders. "First, we throw some light."

Bhayat smiled, saying nothing. He understood.

The older man racked a grenade and counted in his head. He surveyed the horizon, even though it was little more than black. A reflex reaction, and as natural as...

"Now," he said, as the grenade flew into the night sky.

SHADEEB WAS A cautious man, but cold and torpor can dull even the keenest of senses—can blunt even the most finely honed instincts. He had completed another circuit of the encampment, and watched as his counterpart trudged wearily toward him, head turning intermittently to the desert expanse.

Did he look like that? In the unreal green-tinged glow of the monocle, the guard looked less a guard than a sleepwalker. It wouldn't take much to break through a defence that was this close to sleep.

The thought was barely completed before he was aware of the dull *thwump* that came from several hundred yards away. One suppressed fire.

What—

He screamed as the distant green glow became a whiteout that burned into his eyes, searing his retinas and making him claw at the monocle.

His scream was almost—but not quite—loud enough to mask the cough of a suppressed PSG1 on short burst.

JARED GRINNED. "A myth, Matt. That's all it's ever been."

"Maybe," Bolan assented. "But even if these jokers are

charlatans, they've got enough snake oil to fool some smart people. Can't take risks on that. I—"

He stopped suddenly, instinct more than hearing alerting him to the distant sound of a single shot.

Without a word, he uncoiled himself from where he sat cross-legged on the floor of the tent and was halfway toward to the flap, hand reaching for the HK-G3A4 that Jared had supplied him, when the light exploded above them.

THE FLASH GRENADE starred the sky above the camp, turning night to day in an instant. It would alert those in the tents that an attack was underway, but the advantages far outweighed this drawback. The eight attackers finally had illumination to enable them to make their assault. More importantly, the two guards were immobilized by the brilliant light that amplified through the night vision monocles to a point where it blinded them.

As Ali rose from the sand in one sinuous movement and began to move forward quickly, he took in the camp in detail. No one had yet stirred from the tents, and the two guards were bent over, instinctively trying to get their eyes away from the light as they clawed at the monocles, attempting to loosen them and bring their burning retinas some relief.

Ali heard the suppressed crackling of the PSG1 from behind him, and was gratified to see one of the guards spin around and crumple to the sand.

Bhayat was learning. Shoulder and head shot. The guard's kaffiyeh was torn and his head was missing a chunk. Even if the head shot had missed its mark, the shoulder shot would have disabled him until the attack party closed on them. Without knowing if they wore body armor, a body shot was a potentially dangerous waste.

Ali loaded another grenade from the bandolier he wore

under his robes. A magazine was not right for his battle plan. And they had only the one launcher, so it would be best to use sparingly and with thought.

This one would cause collateral damage.

BOLAN EXITED THE tent, the HK ready to fire, muzzle down until an enemy was sighted. His eyes, smarting at the sudden burst of light, squinted to assess the situation. Jared and he were the first out. One guard was on his feet but disabled by his monocle, stumbling blindly and weeping as he tried to adjust his vision.

Dimly, on the periphery of the light horizon, he could see a man standing tall and aiming a grenade launcher.

If they were close enough to open fire, they were within range themselves. As he kept low and sought cover behind one of the jeeps, he raised the HK and judged range and sweep. The G3A4 had a collapsed stock that kept the Uzi copy compact as Bolan swept the horizon with a short burst of fire. As he attained cover he saw the man with the grenade launcher fall back, having taken a hit.

But not before he had managed to loose the grenade toward them. For a moment, Bolan paused with his heart in his throat. The last shot had been a flash to light up the camp— would this be the same? If not, where would it land? In the rapidly dimming light there was no way of telling.

It was with relief that he heard the roar of the exploding grenade about a hundred yards to the right. The impact of the shells that killed his enemy had also deflected his aim. The concussion from the blast was slight, but he still kept his head down and hoped that his comrades did, too—the enemy had chosen a shrapnel grenade, and the metal shards still spattered against the vehicles and tents.

If it had landed on target…

SHADEEB COULDN'T SEE. His eyes were watering and sore beyond any pain he had felt before. Yet he knew that the burst of distant fire had taken out his fellow guard. The sound of ordnance on flesh was distinctive, even without the cry that had been stifled in the throat of the dead man.

They were under attack and it was imperative that he take cover. Both for his own safety and if he was to be of any use. He tried to orient himself and make for the cover of the vehicles or the tents. He was still stumbling when he felt himself grabbed by the arm and hauled down behind a vehicle, jarring a shoulder painfully against the wing of the vehicle.

He blinked. The light overhead was fading rapidly to dark, and this helped his streaming eyes. A blur in front of him was identified by his voice as Jared.

"We're one down and they've got the drop. How many of them and from what direction?"

"I—"

"Never mind, why should you know? Can you see?"

"Barely."

"Okay. Muster the rest. We must assume all points. Got that?"

Shadeeb nodded. He moved toward the tents. Even through his blurred vision he could see that the other men in the encampment were already out of their bivouacs and poised for action. If the fog of sleep had not been shaken by the blasts of fire, then the sudden roar and concussion of a grenade exploding nearby fulfilled the task. As Shadeeb barked at them to fan out and keep down, he felt as though his words were unnecessary. He hunkered down as far toward the center of the camp as he could.

He could defend himself at close range, but that was all. Any attempt to take the offensive would be doomed—he could hardly tell his own men from the enemy. He could easily take out one of his own in error.

Jared was wrong. They were two men down.

BHAYAT WATCHED ALI fall with a mixture of horror and hubris that made for a queasy feeling. He knew the older man thought he was an idiot, but who was still breathing? On the other hand, what the hell should he do next? The soldier who had fired in their direction was in cover. Bhayat sighted through the Hensoldt and got nothing beyond the wing of a jeep. Sweeping the PSG1 around, he got the second guard, presently without his monocle but still stumbling around blindly. He fired a short burst, missing as the man stumbled at a fortuitous moment. The grenade—Ali's last wasted act—had been counterproductive. Instead of being decimated, the enemy had merely been awakened.

Bhayat cursed and lowered the PSG1. The other three attack duos would be moving, and so must he. If nothing else he had to get his hands on the walkie-talkie that Ali still had in his robes. Without it, he was isolated.

Isolated, and with at least one dead shot waiting for him to raise his head.

BOLAN WAITED. ALL around him was chaos as the attack continued from each point of the compass. The chatter of SMG and automatic rifle fire ripped the silence of the desert night. He could hear his people—stirred fully at this point by the near-miss grenade blast—take positions and return the fire that came from out of the night. It was hard to separate the overlapping noise of firearms, but it didn't sound to him as though the attacking force was a large one. At a guess, he'd say four teams of two, one for each compass point, with one of the two due east—and ahead—presently out of the game.

Hassim knew how to pick a team, notwithstanding that

his guards had been caught out. Bolan knew that he could trust them to hold down their ends. His primary task was to take out the second man dead ahead, to ensure that he was immobilized, and was indeed the only other target.

A burst of fire that was wide of him, and missed its intended target, told Bhayat that his opponent was rattled.

In contrast to the firing around the rest of the camp, the silence from dead ahead was overwhelming. A few yards away, just out of cover, Bolan could see the monocle discarded by Shadeeb.

Sighting the direction he had located when the second burst had fired wide, he laid a brief covering fire and darted out, recovering the monocle. Back in cover, he slipped on the night vision equipment; the darkness became greenish, the sand and night sky more clearly delineated. As was the corpse of the man he had taken out—the grenade launcher beside him.

Scanning further back, Bolan could see nothing. If he emerged, he would be exposed. If his opponent was on edge, then perhaps he would make the first move, particularly if he felt the need to back up his compatriots, whose skirmishes lay at Bolan's back. There was urgency there for the soldier—but also for his opponent.

Focusing on the black expanse before him, he used the monocle to scan the horizon. It was no surprise to him when, after a much shorter waiting time than he had feared, a figure rose slowly from out of cover and began to move with stealth toward the prone figure of the soldier Bolan had cut down.

BHAYAT KNEW HE had to move, but fear gripped his bowels and turned them to water. This was his first real taste of combat—the rest had been training, albeit taken seriously enough to kill some—and it was nothing like he had imagined when he had been back home in the First World. He was scared, but he knew that he could not stay immobile.

Ali's corpse had the walkie-talkie. Bhayat would need this to keep contact and link up with his fellows.

If any of them were left. The sound of a firefight from the camp was confusing, but it sounded to him like a hell of a lot more slugs were coming out than going in. And there were no more grenades. Part of the battle plan had been to pepper the camp with CS and shrapnel. Losing Ali had put them down to one grenade launcher—should he try and recover that, as well as the walkie-talkie, then fire one or two in and create some confusion and cover? Where *was* the other grenade launcher and why wasn't it firing?

Hey, if he did that, then maybe, Bhayat figured, he could even come out of this as something of a hero, and not the scared boy he felt at this moment?

A new sense of determination gripped him. He could do this. He considered laying down some covering fire, then realized that this would do little more than reveal his position to the enemy. Feeling as if he had learned something out of all this, he looked to where Ali lay, and taking a deep breath broke his cover, moving across the sand toward the dead man with an awkward slithering shuffle.

He didn't think of his opponent using a monocle. He did not sight through the Hensoldt to take stock of the situation.

Thoughts of glory and victory filled his head. This was not part of the jihad, but the money it would bring would take them one small step further. He was part of that. That was why he had journeyed so far.

He was still thinking of this when he heard a rapid burst of SMG fire that was louder than the rest, and felt almost simultaneously the stitching of pain and liquid fire that blotted out all else.

BOLAN WATCHED HIS man emerge from cover and clumsily move over the sand toward the corpse. It was an easy shot.

There was no time to wonder who these people were and how they had located the camp. That could come later. The threat had be be neutralized.

Bolan flexed his trigger finger, a short burst issued from the HK G3A4. Through the infrared monocle he could see the figure jolt on the surface of the sand then lay still.

He scanned the horizon. All was silent and still. There were two-man parties at each compass point, then, and this sector was secured.

Bolan turned back to the interior of the camp. The tents and vehicles had been tightly clustered. Hassim had questioned why they had pitched fifteen clicks from the oasis itself. The idea had been that they could reach it easily in daylight, but that they would maintain better security at this distance.

That remained to be seen, after this.

There had been fourteen men in their party. One was dead and Shadeeb could be considered inoperative. Twelve men before any other casualties—outnumbering the opposition, if his belief was correct. But the enemy, the cover.

Bolan moved among the men, making a head count as he went. So one man was dead, a head shot having accounted for him. Two more were injured, one in the left leg below the knee, and the other in the right thigh. But both were still firing intermittently.

Bolan came across Hassim, who was hurriedly yelling commands above the noise, directing one of his men to fire a flare above the area to the north in which he had pinpointed enemy fire.

"A little of their own to light the matter up, eh?" Hassim finished as Bolan clapped him on the shoulder.

"Take it to them," Bolan affirmed before briefly outlining what he had gleaned and what he could deduce from the action he had taken. Finishing up, he added, "They either have someone in camp or they have better intel tech than any group around here can easily afford."

Hassim breathed hard. "Never be certain, but I can't see any of these men stooling," he said and then grinned, "like we used to say—good intel, then. If there's as much money and power as you say behind this, then it would be simple to equip more hired hands."

"Hoping you'd say that. C'mon, what's the holdup?" he asked the soldier with the flare.

The response was immediate—a flare shot up into the night, a visible trail tracking its path until it exploded over the northern sector of the desert, lighting it up as though it were day.

Bolan spotted a man with a grenade launcher on his knees. To one side of him, another man with an SMG laid down covering fire. A short tap burst took him out of the equation immediately. The man with the grenade launcher knew that he was as good as dead, but this did not stop him from his task. He pulled the trigger as a barrage of fire cut him down. The grenade may not be true, but his aim was steady enough to ensure that it would still fall within range of the camp.

"Not again," Bolan murmured, unconsciously tensing himself for impact. If it was another shrapnel grenade, or even a Willie Pete, they were in trouble.

But failure was not an option. Not on this night. Not so close to his objective....

3

A few days earlier

Washington had never been Bolan's favorite place. The seat of a government that served the country he loved, and yet it seemed so often to be going against the best interests of the masses. He had found himself in disagreement and conflict so often with government over the years, that he maintained an uneasy truce, looking only to his work on behalf of the people. Trouble was, the government didn't always see it that way—and that had been the cause of a lot of friction over time.

So, if the seat of government was not his favorite place, and he also sought to distance himself physically from Stony Man Farm for many reasons, then where was he supposed to meet with Hal Brognola? True, it was not often that the two had to be in the same physical space to meet and discuss assignments and issues, but still, when the call came they had to meet somewhere.

If nothing else, the big Fed's phone call had been intriguing. First, it had been from an unscrambled and unregistered cell. Second, it had been terse. "We need to meet. Dave Penney's, ten-thirty tonight."

That was all. Bolan's simple query— "Problem?" —had been met with a negative, and then the connection was dead.

It was an interesting call. Rarely would Brognola meet with Bolan outside the Mall when they were both in Washington. And to make it for "Dave Penney's" suggested that Brognola wanted to keep things low-key—for Dave Penney's no longer existed. Once, a long time ago, Penney had owned a junk shop on a remote corner that had fronted for stolen goods and firearms. Bolan had used it back in the day, when he had been forced by circumstance to fly under the radar. Back when Brognola had first known him, and the strong bond but sometimes uneasy alliance between the men had first been forged.

Penney, an Englishman from the north who was hearty, bluff and as hard as a masonry nail, had long since been dispatched to the great beyond by a dissatisfied customer. The lot had been vacant for some years, and then when one of the occasional programs of urban regeneration had taken place, it had been bought, stripped down and refashioned as a diner.

At ten twenty-eight, Bolan stood outside the diner. He had been there an hour earlier, and a half hour after that, passing on the other side of the road—just to be sure.

The diner was called Nighthawks, and the Hopper reference was not so much obvious as blatant. The interior of the diner was lit in a sodium glare that had once been the norm but probably now cost a fortune to replicate. The seats were red and padded, chrome stools lined the counter, and the booths were wood-panelled and covered with black-and-white framed photographs. The booths beside the front window were sporadically full.

But this was not 1942—and it was a long way from Greenwich Village. It had been designed to be a tourist trap, a heritage site to turn a buck. For that, Bolan did not take to it; and yet, for all that, there was something about the nostalgia it inspired that took him back to the root of why he did what he did. What he must. It spoke to him of a childhood and a way of life that was better than the present—certainly in terms of how people treated each other. Sure, much of it was a fantasy—as much as the diner that turned his thoughts this way—but it was an aspiration and belief that had carried him through his life.

What were the chances that Brognola knew this? He knew that Bolan would remember Penney's, and that he would both love and hate what had been done to the old place. He would appreciate the irony, too.

While this crossed his mind, he scoped the block. There was no sign it was being watched. If Brognola had been worrying about being tailed, then he had avoided any attempt to do so.

Bolan went inside. The night outside had been cool. Inside, the diner was warm in that way that only a short-order joint can be. He felt perspiration break out on his forehead as he stepped up to the counter and ordered black coffee.

"Anything else I can get for you?" The middle-aged, plump blonde smiled. Her uniform was forties-style, and was tight at the seams. Her smile took your attention away from that.

"Maybe. I'm waiting for someone—no, he's here," he added, spotting Brognola sitting in a booth in the far corner, two seats from the men's room. Close enough to make an exit, far enough to react if trouble came the other way.

"I'll come over in a few minutes, hon. You take a seat," the waitress said as she poured the steaming coffee.

Bolan thanked her and walked over to where Brognola was seated. The big Fed was staring at an omelet and didn't look up as Bolan took the seat opposite.

"It's changed, Striker. Not, maybe, for the better."

"I don't know." Bolan sipped his coffee. "Better than Dave used to provide. Always the aftertaste of gun oil."

"Penney was for real—better or worse. You can't go back." Brognola picked at his omelet with a fork.

"So, is this about one of those, of the homeland?" Bolan asked.

"Both. Order something, but not omelet," Brognola murmured as the waitress approached. Bolan ordered cherry pie. It seemed somehow appropriate.

When the waitress had delivered his order and they were left alone, Bolan took up the thread. "Why here?"

"You would know the location. Didn't want to meet you on the Mall. Too many eyes and ears, even friendly ones. Ever hear of cold fusion?"

"Nuclear, right?" Bolan queried.

Brognola assented. "Small-scale stuff when it was stumbled on, and highly contentious."

"This would be—what—late eighties, right?"

"To begin with, though things haven't been as quiet as you might think since then. It started with a couple of electrochemists who had a weird by-product from an experiment. Fleischmann and Pons—"

"Out to make a name or already had one?"

"Oh, they had a name alright, and a lot to lose if they got it wrong. Anyhow, they found that in one of their experiments they were producing an amount of heat that they couldn't explain. It was about the electrolysis of heavy water and some kind of element. I'm not a scientist—"

"You're doing okay so far," Bolan said. "How big was this experiment?"

"Just another experiment, nothing with any big research or kudos attached. The point about it was that they couldn't explain the heat in any other way than some kind of nuclear fusion reaction within the cells. And it was a small experiment—I mean, they were doing this on a tabletop in a lab, for Chrissakes—and if you extrapolate from that...."

"You come to a way of making energy cheaply and easily, with presumably little risk to health."

"Exactly. Fusion is far safer than fission, but expensive—very expensive. Whereas this experiment would make it cheap and easily accessible."

Bolan sat back. "That would have made it a very valuable piece of information. But we're not powering cities off of lab tables, are we? So what went wrong?"

"The DOE—the Department of Energy—had a commission to look into this at the time. They came to the conclusion that there was some evidence—enough to support a modest program—but not enough to pour vast resources into this pigeon, in case it stiffed. Fifteen years later they had another commission, and came up with the same conclusion."

"Do the *standing still,* right? It's that nice little governmental dance where no one gets caught out."

Brognola shrugged. "Maybe. I don't know enough about the science to say for sure. But I've been doing a bit of research, and a lot of people do take it seriously, and we're not talking cranks here. Thing is, there had been some talk about it sixty years before, but it was all just talk. Then, when Fleishmann and Pons did it, they rushed publishing the results because of pressure from their employers. Even academics need to generate cash."

"So I'm guessing here that there was a lot of dissent."

The big Fed grinned. "Hell, yeah. The number of people who tried to replicate the experiment and then didn't. There was a point where Fleischmann and Pons were being ridiculed. Then it went quiet, which always suggests that someone, somewhere has found something out."

"Y'know, this is fascinating, Hal, but I'm having trouble seeing what this has to do with calling me down to a place that I used to know a long time ago under another guise. Or, if it comes to that, what a bunch of scientists and test tubes has to do with the line of work I'm in."

"I'm coming to that, Striker. You need the background to understand why it's important, and why it has to be this way."

"Okay, carry on," Bolan assented.

Brognola looked up to the ceiling of the diner. "You would think, given that it was a discredited theory, that it would just fade into history. But it didn't. There were sporadic pieces of individual research, and more importantly, the Japanese poured in a lot of time and money between 1992 and 1997—a good few years after the initial wave. Then they came back to it in '08. The Indian government carried on research into the early nineties, then ceased until a few years back, when they got interested again."

"What about our boys?"

Brognola smiled. "Ah, that's where it gets interesting. We were carrying on research from the late eighties until 2002 at the Space and Naval Warfare Systems Center in San Diego. Nothing conclusive surfaced, but I'll tell you something— last year NASA Langley Research Center announced that they were starting up a research program that had already yielded interesting results."

"Hey, that's smart—getting results before you even start." Bolan grinned. "Our boys at NASA are better than we thought. So it's not a dead duck and it looks like it could go places. The problem is *what,* exactly?"

"The problem is that there are a lot of nations that haven't been doing this kind of research, but would seriously love to jump on the bandwagon. If this really does have substance, then think about what it would mean."

"Not weapons. Fusion doesn't give you the by-products for warheads. But it would mean cheap power easily sourced. That's no bad thing, surely?"

"In a humanitarian sense, no—not if it was open to all.

But what if it was just auctioned to the highest bidder? Then they would have complete control and could sell it on at a named price. Or maybe they could keep it from the nations that were not their allies, or refused to toe the line. Or maybe, if they had a vested interest in fossil fuel, they could keep it under wraps so that they could wring out a few more dollars before the gravy train runs out. Whatever the reason, if it went to one nation against the rest, then it could raise some serious issues."

"If we have it, and the Japanese are still interested, then what—"

"We're not there yet. I'm pretty sure the Japanese aren't, either. But there is someone who claims they have it. They've got proof that's convincing enough."

Bolan was silent for a moment. Finally, he said, "Right. And that would be where I come in." He raised a hand as Brognola made to speak. "Wait a second—we've been sitting here too long without cause." He indicated the waitress, who had been eyeing them with interest.

He beckoned her over, ordered more coffee for himself and Brognola, and used the opportunity to take in the rest of the diner. Most of the people who had been seated when he arrived were now gone. Very few had replaced them—some obvious tourists and two men in dark suits who had seated themselves at a window booth. They were not speaking and both stared out of the window.

"I wonder how long they've been there," Bolan said softly, with the ghost of a smile.

"I think since I reached the part where the Japanese got interested."

"No worries. We'll just settle the tab and take a little walk. I get the idea there's more to this."

"Exactly," Brognola said.

They finished up their coffee quickly, and Bolan paid at

the counter while Brognola waited. Bolan noticed that the big Fed was without a briefcase or notes of any kind—everything he had to say was in his head. That was unlike him.

Thanking the waitress, Bolan indicated to Brognola to follow him. They left the diner without a glance at the two men seated in the window booth. Bolan, did, however, cast a surreptitious eye over them from the outside. Underarm holsters. Discreet but still noticeable earpieces—linked to a listening device? They couldn't have bugged the diner but they might have a scanner. Assume that. One thing was for sure—they were making no attempt to hide themselves, and in fact acted like they wanted to be seen.

Bolan guided Brognola down the street, hanging first left and then right. He was walking with a casual gait that belied its speed.

"Are we actually trying to lose them?" the big Fed asked.

"I don't think that would be feasible. They probably have communications open, and they want us to see them. I don't want to risk them overhearing through any means what you have to say next."

Brognola said no more, preferring to save his breath. He showed no surprise when Bolan cornered again, then hauled him into a narrow alley between two buildings. They had moved away from the main drag and were in an area that was growing more deserted as the hour grew late.

"What if we've already lost them?" Brognola whispered.

Bolan smiled mirthlessly. "You really think I would let that happen?"

Brognola knew the answer, and did not bother to respond. Instead, he waited for a few moments. Then, as he had suspected would happen, the two suited men walked past, their pace between hurry and panic. Bolan mouthed "wait" and moved behind them, falling into step so that his footfalls would not echo out of time and so alert them.

This had to be quick. The street was empty and the buildings around had blank windows that did not betray habitation.

In four steps Bolan had caught up with the two men. One blow to the base of the neck sent the man on the right tumbling forward, stumbling before hitting the sidewalk. The man on the left half turned, flinging out an arm in a swinging chop. He was too slow to react. Bolan had already sidestepped, and jabbing a punch at the base of the jaw that snapped the man's head back, sending his earpiece skittering across the Tarmac of the road.

Before he had a chance to react, a second blow rendered the man unconscious. Before he had even hit the sidewalk, Bolan had stepped forward to drag the first man upright by his collar. Another swift jab to the point of the jaw also rendered him unconscious. Bolan still had him, sagging, by the collar, as he looked back to see Brognola peering from out of the alley.

Beckoning him, Bolan took better hold of the man in his grasp and dragged him back toward the alley. Taking his cue, Brognola came forward and lifted the other man off the sidewalk, puffing slightly as he dragged him backward in Bolan's wake.

Once in the alley, he laid his burden down beside the man that Bolan was already searching. Without a word, Bolan moved across and searched the second man. Looking up at Brognola, he shook his head, then beckoned that the big Fed should follow him. He did not speak until they had walked, briskly, at least a hundred yards.

"Nothing on them. I guess we should assume they're ours. So why did you want to meet me out here? Who has the ears you didn't want hearing this?"

"We're black, right?"

"None more so."

"Yeah, well, that's not the case. There are others who have a shade of black that would suck the light out of you."

"They have an interest in cold fusion?"

"It's partly the science. Mostly who the interested parties are and how it's being sold. It might suit them to let this go ahead."

"But it wouldn't suit you?" Bolan asked.

"Or you. The greater good. I might be a cynical old bastard who's been in this job too long, but I haven't forgotten why I signed up. And neither have you. The Supreme Commander may not even know about a lot of these blacker-than-black teams. I don't, come to that. I just suspect."

"And things happen that add some fuel to that suspicion."

"Right. Striker, just where the hell are we going?"

Bolan chuckled. While they had been talking, he had been leading Brognola across blocks and down streets that the big Fed did not recognize. They were in areas where his suit—and even Bolan's chinos and black sweater—seemed conspicuously out of place.

"Off the beaten track, Hal, somewhere where they might not think to look."

Brognola shrugged, and allowed Bolan to lead him through a maze of streets until they came to a small basement bar. Descending the steps and entering the stuffy heat of the interior, Brognola had to adjust to the dim lighting and the blare of the wall-mounted TV that pounded out a ball game.

"Hey, Cooper—I thought you wasn't going to show your face after the Red Sox. You still owe me twenty on that."

"Tiny, I always pay my debts. I was just out of town." Bolan peeled off two twenties. "Beer, scotch, and one for yourself."

"Apology accepted," Tiny acknowledged. At over six and half feet and around three hundred pounds, the nickname was inevitable. He poured the drinks, handed over a fistful of change, raised a glass to his benefactor and turned his attention back to the screen.

Bolan handed Brognola the Scotch and indicated a table against the far wall. The two men seated themselves, Brognola leaned over the table so that he could be heard without yelling too loudly.

"Nice place. You come here often?"

"Often enough to lose too many bets on games to that big lug," Bolan replied. "It helps to have somewhere out of the way. I'll bet that even with the intel you have, you didn't know about this place."

Brognola shrugged. "Nothing personal, it's just that we need to know where our people can be found."

"Right. Bear will be breaking a sweat trying to figure out how I kept this quiet."

"I won't tell him. After all, you won't be here again after tonight."

"Right. But for now, it's secure. So why don't you fill me in on what you want me to do?"

"Here?"

Bolan looked around. The bar was half-full, and the majority of the customers were gathered toward the end of the bar where the ball game was loudly claiming their attention. Of those who were not paying attention, most were in heated and absorbed conversation, with only a few staring morosely into their drinks.

"You think of anywhere that we're less likely to be listened in on?"

Brognola paused, and then shrugged. "Got me there. It goes down like this. A very simple, businesslike email starts making the rounds. Just like any email scam. Except that this is no ordinary piece of spam. It only goes into the inboxes of those with power and influence. And, maybe more importantly, whoever sent it also knew who these people had on their books as consultants, because it lands in the inboxes of those people, too. Scientists who would know Shinola from the more dubious alternative. So the powerful and influential talk to their consultants, and they figure that this is worth a response, all the while getting their other consultants—the security ones—to try and follow up on where the email came from."

"Except the IT crowd find that the address and IP are extremely well hidden and have a trail that peters out to nowhere."

"Exactly." Brognola sipped his Scotch and made a wry face. "You don't come here to drink, do you? No, perhaps not," he added, noting that Bolan was nursing rather than drinking his beer. He continued: "So those with power and influence speak to those they have power and influence over, and they listen. They like what they hear. A simple affirmative is returned to the inbox of the "company" concerned, and they are told to wait for instructions."

"The powerful and influential, Hal—who do they wield this influence with?"

"We know of several small nations from the old Soviet Bloc. For those on the African and Asian continents, it would provide them with a source of power and independence that would be invaluable. For those in the Middle East it could be a way of keeping some control over fossil fuel prices. As for the Chinese…well, no one's too sure about what they've achieved, but keeping things sewn up would always benefit them."

"I get it. It could be a free-for-all. So how do I fit into this?"

"We know that the auction is to be held in the Middle East. Invitation only. Small teams from each bidder. The location is to be kept secret until the last moment, to avoid interference."

"I'd like to see how they plan to do that. Every bidder is going to have a team ready to go in and wipe out the opposition if they don't come out on top."

"That's my concern. If that happens, then we end up with a very confusing bloodbath on soil that lies in a very contentious zone. You can bet your ass that we'll have people there, from an unidentified and unidentifiable agency. If they get caught up in this, they'll be the ones assigned culpability."

"That's one thing we've had enough of in that region," Bolan agreed. "Your point is well taken. Am I right in assuming that this will be an unknown quantity, even to Stony Man?"

"You can get intel, but the purpose of that intel—"

Bolan smiled. "Bear will love that. It'll drive him even more crazy than knowing about this place. So my job is to get in…and then what?"

"Stop the auction."

"Hal, there's going to be enough hardware and personnel around there for a medium-sized army."

Brognola grinned. "There won't be an auction to stop if you secure the merchandise."

"You want me to find the formula?"

Brognola shook his head. "The auction will be for the scientists. They'll be there like it's some kind of old-fashioned slave market. Which it is, I guess. Some things never really change."

"And that, of course, makes it easier," Bolan said with a wry grin. He looked over the bar. "I wouldn't like to bet with Tiny on this one. When and where do I start?"

"Syria." Brognola reached into his jacket. "I got you a ticket."

4

Bolan took a scheduled flight to Damascus using the ticket Brognola had given him. Raiding a war chest, he made sure that he had currency. He would need it when he landed, as he was forced to travel without any kind of armory. It had been a while since he was in that part of the globe, but some things carry on regardless of political climate.

Like all of the major cities in the country, Damascus had been hit by the unrest and uprising. And like the rest of the major cities, it had come under the heel of the military. Time and again. Presently, there was an uneasy peace in the streets as Bolan checked into a hotel as Matt Cooper. If anyone from another black ops team was looking for him and suspected Brognola had sent him, he would be easy to find. That might not be a bad thing—it was pretty safe to assume that Brognola's actions had been noted. It might draw some people from the woodwork and give Bolan the chance to make a few intel connections. He wouldn't be here long. Certainly not long enough for anyone to pose a danger to him.

Registering with nothing more than a small gym bag had not raised the eyebrows at the hotel that it had at the American end of the flight. Different circumstances bred different expectations: this could work to his advantage.

After a quick shower to wash off the torpor of travel, Bolan hit the streets. He carried the handgrip with him. Nothing much had changed in terms of the architecture and layout since his last visit. He just hoped that this lack of change would be mirrored by those who lived in the buildings. A brief cab ride dropped him five minutes from his intended destination. He made the rest of the journey on foot, through backstreet stone buildings shaded from the heat and under awnings that were tattered and ripped, hanging over the streets and side alleys at unkempt and uncared-for angles.

No matter where in the world he was, or what the style of building may be, there was a feeling about these places that never changed. He stood in front of a wooden door that was thick, scarred and pitted, and looked bleached by time and the elements.

It hadn't changed in all these years. When he banged on the door, the small spy hole in the door opened. A wrinkled face that was as pitted and scarred as the door looked out at him. At first suspicious, it took a moment for Bolan's identity to register, then the face became wreathed in a smile.

"Belasko, you remembered your old friend after so long."

"Hadez, I was never your friend, but my cash may have been."

"You carry the money, you are my friend. But what are you doing standing there? You must come in."

"I would be only too pleased, but first…" He indicated the door, still closed, that stood between them.

Hadez opened the door and ushered Bolan inside. Once the door was closed behind him, Bolan found himself in a cool stone room that was dimly lit. As his eyes adjusted, he could see that the chairs, hangings and low tables remained almost as he remembered them from long ago. If the layers of dust on them were anything to go by, they had lain unused for the whole time. But then, Hadez had priorities other than housework, particularly in a part of the house that mattered little to him.

"I take it that my friend does not visit me after so many years purely because he has missed my company in sudden recollection?"

"You would be correct. And it's not Mr. Belasko these days, Hadez. I prefer to answer to Cooper. That's what it says on my credit cards, though I doubt you would take them."

Hadez was a man as wizened and bent as his face would suggest. He made a gesture that could have been a shrug. "I prefer it when there is not trail of paper to be followed. That was always how it was, and I see no reason to change a good habit."

"I couldn't agree more. You know why I am here. I find myself indisposed when I would rather not be. Perhaps you can be of assistance."

"Anything for such an old and valued friend. Please, this way."

With a sweep of his arm, he indicated that Bolan should take the curtained doorway ahead of them. It led to a flight of stone stairs lit by a string of lights with a reinforced door at the bottom. Squeezing past Bolan, Hadez unlocked the door and let the soldier into the storeroom where he kept his merchandise.

"It's nice to see that you can still rely on some things." Bolan smiled as he surveyed the crates and boxes stacked against the walls. "I'm pretty sure you'll have exactly what I'm looking for."

"If you have a list for the market, I will do my best to comply," Hadez said with a slight bow.

"Let's begin with small arms and work our way up," Bolan began.

An hour and a half later, having haggled over the price with the vendor as was expected, Bolan packed two duffel bags with the ordnance he had purchased and was ready to leave.

"What's it like on the streets these days?" he asked.

Hadez shrugged. "These are difficult times, my friend. But I think I know what you ask. Yes, the military are more alert than in previous times, and not as susceptible to the lure of the bribe. It makes my business more difficult in many ways, but do not worry, I have trustworthy drivers who know the areas to avoid. Come, I will assist you—no extra charge."

"Your generosity knows no bounds," Bolan said, straight-faced.

The old merchant said nothing, but allowed himself a small smile before pulling a cell phone from his pocket and hitting a speed-dial number. When his call was answered he spoke rapidly, pausing only briefly and not allowing whoever was on the other end of the line to speak more than a few phrases. With a firm nod, he ended the call and looked at Bolan.

"My man will be out front in six minutes exactly. He will take you wherever you wish to go, and ensure that you reach your destination without any interference."

Bolan assented wordlessly. He had feigned ignorance through the call, keeping his face a slightly puzzled mask. He had never spoken in an Arabic language to Hadez, allowing the man to believe that he could only converse in English. This was not entirely true. Although the soldier's grasp of the language was rusty, and the old man spoke rapidly in a thick dialect, he had been able to pick out enough to know that safe conduct was only part of the deal. The driver would report back on the destination and also tail him.

Why not? The old man lived in dangerous times, in a perilous place, and in an uncertain industry. A little knowledge would be useful. Bolan had no doubt that Hadez would not use any information gleaned on customers without due need—anything else would be impolitic—but Bolan could do without his movements being known.

The driver was on time to the second. Hadez kept that time on an old pocket watch that was affectation, and when it hit the mark he indicated that Bolan should leave. Shouldering his duffel bags, Bolan exited the building as a battered Fiat drew up at the end of the alley.

"May your God go with you," Hadez said with a bow.

"And with you," Bolan returned as he exited, adding to himself that there was no way any god would find out his destination from the driver.

Bundling himself into the rear of the vehicle, he settled as the driver pulled out into the road, peering over his shoulder and almost colliding with another vehicle as he did so.

"So where you wanna go, boss?" the driver asked, his face fat, sweaty and disingenuous.

"Take me to the airport," he said flatly.

The driver looked puzzled, wiping sweat from his eyes with one hand, the other on the wheel that he seemed to turn arbitrarily.

"You kidding me, boss? Army got that tight. You go there after where you been, you ain't getting on no plane."

"That's my worry," Bolan answered. "You just get me there in one piece."

The driver shrugged as he turned his attention back to the road, cursing loudly at a cyclist he sent tumbling into the curb. Bolan sat back in the cracked leatherette seat, pondering his next course of action.

It had never been his intention to return to his hotel. It had served his purpose as a place to register and clean up. If anyone knew of his arrival, they would have perhaps tailed him from there—although he was sure that he had been tail free—or at the very least would have a location for him. Let them wait. While he was here, he had no intention of standing still long enough to be tagged.

The Fiat skewed into the road approaching the airport.

The driver had said nothing else, but must have been wondering if the American was crazy enough to try and get on or charter a plane while carrying that much hardware.

Bolan had no intention of leaving Damascus yet, but if Hadez believed that to be the case, so much the better.

The Fiat pulled in front of the airport. Soldiers and armed police were heavily visible. The driver eyed them nervously. He had no intention of being picked up with a passenger so heavily laden—which was kind of what Bolan counted on. He eased himself out of the vehicle.

"I'll take it from here," he said blandly. "Give Hadez my regards, and don't park here too long—it's only a dropping zone."

He shouldered the duffel bags and took a couple of steps away from the vehicle, not looking back. He heard the driver grind the Fiat into gear and screech off from behind him; a couple of the armed police had already been eyeing the Fiat as it hesitated.

The same officers watched him as he entered the airport building. For his part, Bolan remained impassive. If they stopped him, it was a problem. But only if. He kept walking—past the check-in desks, past the bar and toward the men's room. Over his shoulder he could feel the eyes of the police officers follow him, and as he neared the washroom, he slid into a crowd. Security cameras could follow him, but not the naked eye.

Another exit beckoned and he switched direction, hailing a cab and climbing into it swiftly. He gave the name of his hotel and breathed a sigh of relief as the cab exited the airport. Checking, he couldn't see a tail.

He pulled out his smartphone. There were emails from Brognola, as promised. One contained the note that had first been circulated concerning the auction, which he skimmed. It told him little more than he already knew. A second email gave details of the location, time and date. So he had this, but in truth it counted for little. Someone would know that Brognola was harvesting this information, and that it was being passed on. He had little doubt that it could be traced to him—information tech was useful, but he had no faith in its security. It put him on par with those who sought to buy in terms of intel, but otherwise he would have to use his own skills to stay one jump ahead, and chances were that it would be changed. As long as Brognola could update him, then fine.

Bolan leaned over and asked the driver to change destination. "I need to do something before I check in." He gave an address around the block from Hadez's domain. The old man wouldn't expect him to be so close, and it somewhat amused Bolan to hide in such plain sight.

He thrust a bundle of cash at the driver. "Wait for me."

Leaving the cab running at the roadside, Bolan walked down an alley and out of the cab driver's world. The man could wait there as long as he liked before giving up—there was plenty of cash to recompense him.

The streets and alleys in this quarter were winding and mazelike—presumably why Hadez still felt so at home and safe amongst them. But not much had changed in the years since Bolan's last visit, and he was soon able to locate a café that was still in business. Entering, he ordered coffee and took a seat as far away from the bar as possible. The café was almost empty, just the proprietor and a middle-aged man with a weather-beaten and scarred visage present. His coffee in front of him, the duffel bags and holdall safely stashed beneath his table, Bolan hit a number on his speed dial.

"Striker… Interesting location from GPS, and not a secured line at present. Give me a second…" Bolan waited patiently through a series of barely audible hisses and clicks, then: "Well, Hal said we'd be hearing from you soon enough, but he wasn't exactly forthcoming."

"Not sure that there's much I can add at the moment, Bear. I need some intel from you. Maps, topography. I'll send you the locations. But more than that, I'm on my own here, and I'll need some backup. A man on the ground who knows the territory and can be relied on to put together a team."

There was a brief moment's silence. Bolan could visualize Aaron "The Bear" Kurtzman, in his wheelchair, mind working faster than his fingers as they flew across a keyboard. Even with touch-screens, Kurtzman worked faster on keys, as if the motion helped speed his mind.

"I have someone, Striker. Jared Hassim. Rogue from us after a spell in Afghanistan. Deep cover that some say went a little too deep. To be frank, looking at his record and what we have on him, I'd say it was more a case of him being disillusioned with all parties and figuring that he'd be better as a freelancer."

"Great, I love freebooters," Bolan said wryly.

"This one is a little different. No record of him ever landing one of his own in deep. Actually looks reliable."

"Jared…" Bolan's mind traveled back a few years to his brief foray into the Afghan territories. Then back before that: to West Point and a man in uniform he had never expected to see again. "I know him. Not well. But we've crossed paths a couple of times."

"His details are on their way to you, along with the requested intel. Anything else you need right now?"

Bolan thought about it. "No. If I do, then I'll call. I don't have much to go on at my end, and what I do have is probably compromised. This one will have to be close."

"Okay, Striker. You know where I am."

"Thanks." Bolan disconnected, and then brought up the intel that Kurtzman had sent—background on Jared Hassim. He had been a UCLA political student, athlete, West Point grad and a U.S. Marine with a good record. He had also converted to Islam eighteen months before 9/11. Recruited into black ops immediately after the event, having been singled out as religious but not fundamentalist, he received further training and was sent to Afghanistan to work in deep cover with the Taliban. His age had been to his advantage then, as he had been seen as an elder with experience. A useful soldier, he was also a man of conscience with a deep vein of individuality and stubbornness. It seemed that disgust at both sides, and the knowledge that this was becoming apparent, had fuelled a move into the realms of the freelancer. He had settled in Damascus five years back and lived on the other side of the city.

Bolan checked the time. Less than thirty-six hours until the auction; he would have to move quickly. Finishing his coffee, he collected his baggage and made for the door, muttering thanks to the proprietor and the old man who sat by the bar, grumbling to the proprietor in an undertone.

He set off on foot, checked for a tail and then picked up a cab. Traffic through the city center was heavy as the hour progressed, and he became bogged down in a morass of trucks, cars and bikes that sought to gain an advantage on streets where traffic regulations were an unknown quantity. Using the time to acquaint himself with the location for the auction, he knew that he would have to persuade Hassim quickly or else set off on his own. He had a long way to travel, and it would help if he had a local man to gain the transport needed, if not the manpower he would prefer.

Latakia was a Mediterranean port, a city and governerate of half a million people, and—more importantly—two, maybe three districts away. To get to it would entail a roundabout road route or a hop across a bay that was inevitably heavily guarded. This was before the mission could even be mounted—that would present a whole other series of issues. Bolan hoped that this wouldn't be symptomatic of the mission as a whole.

As the cab ground its way through the traffic he sat back and considered his position. If Brognola was right, even elements of the U.S. government would be at this auction. He could not rely on any backup, and knew that Stony Man could be compromised if he put a foot wrong. It would be best if he kept contact to a minimum.

The cab driver pulled across the road, ignoring the blaring horns and curses that rained on him, and turned to Bolan. He grunted the fare amount, and took the money with little sign of interest in anything other than his passenger's billfold.

As he pulled away, leaving Bolan standing outside a shop where fruit and vegetables tumbled off makeshift tables into the late-afternoon sun, the soldier wondered what reception he would receive.

He stepped into the shadows of the shop interior. It seemed deserted, but the hairs on his neck prickled nonetheless.

"Mr. Belasko. Long time. No offence, but if you'd put down those bags very slowly and raise your arms above your head, I won't have to shoot you."

5

"I wonder if they realize what this will mean to them," Roman Bosnich murmured as he sipped his iced tea.

"I suspect that if they did, they would not have been so willing to throw their lot in with us," his companion replied, stirring the dissolving sugar cube around the small glass of Turkish—and therefore boiling—tea.

"Hadji, you surprise me sometimes with your innocence. I wonder if it could become a liability."

"They are scientists. Worldly things mean little to them."

Bosnich chuckled, shaking his head. "Science demands money in order to perpetuate its experiments. The fact that they could not gain legitimate funding, and that they worked in an area considered fringe science, caused them the requisite distress looking for a sponsor. They were not fussy where that sponsor's funds may come from. It's all about money, and all about greed, Hadji. It's just the things that motivate that greed that differ. Offer them the chance to live in their own bubble, continuing their own experiments to their hearts' content, and they would sell their own grandmothers at auction." His face hardened. "They are like everyone else. They have a price, and when offered that price they do not think of consequences."

"Then, if they do not think of the consequences, my point remains." His companion shrugged. "If they had…"

Bosnich shrugged also, unconcerned. "They would. They would consider it worth it. They would consider any price as worth it. They are as driven as anyone else."

"Maybe… Still, they shall not be our responsibility for much longer. I wonder if that has even crossed their minds?"

"I doubt it. They are more likely to be wondering when they can begin to use the new facilities that we promised them."

"That rather depends on how far the winning bidder has to transport them, doesn't it," Harinder Singh, the man known to Bosnich as Hadji, mused. He looked down from the bridge of the yacht to where the two men in question reclined on sun loungers. They were pale—one middle-aged, the other just edging out of youth—and they seemed uneasy, almost unable to relax—unlike Singh or Bosnich. Both were traders in arms who had, in recent years, expanded their trade to encompass manpower as much as hardware. Brokers in commodities, they preferred to think of themselves. As such, when they had heard of two scientists claiming to have made significant progress in cold fusion they had—once they had checked what this actually entailed—realized that here was a commodity outside the norm but that may prove to be profitable.

The man who had told them of the scientists was small-time. He had been approached through a third party. The kind of funding the men were looking for was outside his remit, but for an introductory fee—extracted from both sides, naturally—he had been able to arrange a meeting.

Bosnich and Singh knew that they had many contacts, all of whom would see the advantages in buying these talents and this information. For the traders, there was the additional knowledge that money saved in one budget would, in many cases, find its way into an arms budget from which they could also profit further.

A win/win situation. With introductions effected, it was

simple for them to set the men up with a lab in their Swiss homeland where they could produce enough proof to justify both the investment of time and money, and also provide ample material for a prospectus. The scientists thought it would be for funding purposes to produce under contract—but the traders knew it would be a simple bill of sale. Everything—man, lab and findings—would be shipped to their new owners like a crate of knock-off AK-47s. Except, of course, at a much greater profit...

The scientists had been moved from their Swiss base some two days before, and as far as they were concerned would attend a series of funding meetings where they would demonstrate their findings. They did not know that even as they lay at uneasy rest on the sun deck of the yacht, their lab had been dismantled and carefully packed, ready to be transported to their new home at a moment's notice. Both men were single, which had greatly simplified matters—not that a family could not as easily be packed up, or disposed of.

The yacht *Taurus* had been moored in the harbour at Latakia for a little over twenty-four hours. Money had changed hands in order for it to be officially invisible, but bribery had a statute of limitations. Despite his casual air, Bosnich would be glad when the next day had come, and they could complete the sale before leaving with a haste that others—but not he—would consider undue.

Singh, on the other hand, despite his idle musing, had less conscience than curiosity, and was prepared to invest as much in payments to officials as would be necessary. Unlike his partner, he felt any threat would not be official, but rather from other traders wishing to take a piece of the action.

Neither man had figured on a third option.

Singh sipped at his sweet, scalding tea. In the heat of late afternoon it felt cool, a paradox he enjoyed, as he did the presence of their 165-foot pleasure vessel in a harbor otherwise alive with working boats. Despite the incongruity, he noted that they were not the subject of curiosity. The strangeness of their presence was warning enough. He said as much to Bosnich.

"Hadji, your sense of irony will get you into trouble one day. I just hope it doesn't drag me with it. We have some work still to do. Besides, I think the merchandise is getting nervous with the way it is being watched."

He gave the two men on the sun deck a brief wave and smile before leading his grinning companion down below to finalize the auction arrangements.

"I WOULD LIKE this more if we had not had to leave our work," Tomas Gabriel grumbled as he sat huddled on a sun lounger. His posture would have been more appropriate if they had been in a colder region, but nonetheless reflected his sense of unease.

"Tom, you worry too much." Uli Hoeness reclined and looked up to the bridge, acknowledging Bosnich before he and the other man disappeared. "You know why we need to be here. We secure the funding, we go home, we work again. Meantime, you should relax. You're still young and have your career before you. Mine is past its peak."

"You make it sound as if I am carrying you. That's not convincing. Neither are you in any other way. Look at the way you are sitting. You act like you are relaxed, but I have seen teak and oak with more flexibility than you."

"Perhaps I am nervous." Hoeness cast his eye over the men who discreetly ringed the deck. They were armed, but their armaments were unobtrusive and hidden—Bosnich and Singh thought that he did not notice this. They did not know everything about him and his previous work. True, Syria had been experiencing unrest: but were they there to protect the two scientists or to contain them?

"Perhaps I am nervous," he stated again in a stronger voice, not wishing to alarm his already rattled companion. "But if I am, it is only because I fear that those who have the finances will not fully understand us."

"Ah, yes," Gabriel muttered darkly. "But if they do not, what will our current benefactors do about that? They are not philanthropists, I think."

"No. No, I don't suppose they are," Hoeness said softly.

"YOUR CAUTION DOES you credit, Jared. But you obviously remember me. Unless you have a hotline to Hadez."

"So that's where you got this junk?" Hassim answered as he rooted through the duffel bags that he had made Bolan kick across the floor.

"Not for the money I paid. Not with his reputation, either." Bolan eyed the scrawny kid who was covering him with an HK MP5. He was no more than fifteen, but his eyes were glittering and cold. Too far to reach before he could trigger a burst, and he wouldn't hesitate—of that, Bolan was sure.

"Why would he think you were coming to me? You say anything? Ask any questions?"

"Why would I do that? At the outside, knowing your background—and I assume he would—and knowing mine, he might just add it up. But I doubt that. You used a name—same as him—that I haven't used for a long time now. And I remember you."

Hassim looked up from the duffel bags. For a moment there was a faraway look in his eye. "You do, do you? That's interesting. Man like you must work alongside a lot of guys. Most of them probably dead by now, too."

"You're not. That makes you memorable."

"Because I remember how to stay alive?"

"It's a skill worth acquiring, and one that's good to have on your side."

Hassim moved the bags behind him, further out of reach. The interior of the store was musty and dark, smelling of vegetables and fruit that had been stored too long. Tables and benches covered in produce lined the side walls. At the back was a doorway covered by a rug pinned above the lintel. The boy squatted on a chair to one side of the door. Hassim stood to the other. If the boy hadn't been there, his squat, grizzled appearance would have led you to believe he could be nothing more than a grocer.

"Why would I want to be on your side, Mr. Cooper?"

"Be nice and you can call me Matt."

"Matt, then. Why would I want to be on anyone's side? I retired from that game a long time ago. Your intel must have told you that."

"Sure looks like you retired," Bolan said wryly, indicating the boy and his MP5.

"These are dangerous times, Matt. Everyone needs a little security."

"Well, you've looked in those bags, and you can see the kind of security you could buy. That's just the down payment. I need men who know the area and know how to fight. I need them quick. I know I can trust you."

Hassim looked at him quizzically. Bolan sighed.

"You're a professional. Your record says that you take that seriously. I pay you and you'll take that as a responsibility. Besides which, if you really do like living here, you might not want the balance of power to shift. It could make things difficult for a man who just wants to sell a few vegetables."

"Now you have me interested," Hassim said. He gestured to the boy, barked a few words in an Arabic dialect Bolan could not follow. The boy jumped off the chair, hooking the leg with his foot so that it spun toward the soldier across the floor. All the while he kept the MP5 leveled at Bolan.

"Take a seat, Matt. Tell me more…."

THREE HOURS LATER, darkness enveloped Damascus as Hassim marshalled his men into the small back room. It was lit by an oil lamp that smoked and stank almost as badly as the smell of their sweat as they congregated in the confined space. Apprehension—it was like fear, but not as rank. Twelve men jammed in alongside Hassim and Bolan in the crowded space.

Hassim spoke to them in their own language. Bolan could follow parts of it, and was amused to find himself described as an American but not an imperialist, and as a pirate with plenty of cash to throw around.

"You understand," he continued smoothly in English as he turned to the soldier, "that in a country where any kind of travel can be subject to a warrant, the idea of a few extra shekels to oil the wheels of that travel can only be seen as a good thing."

"Of course. And distancing myself from the U.S. military can do no harm."

"In the current climate the only thing worse than an American soldier is a Syrian soldier, my friend."

Bolan assented. "Understandable, I guess… Now, to matters at hand." He scanned the group clustered in the room. "How many of you speak good English?" There was an uneasy silence. "I ask because I want you to understand clearly, and my Arabic is rusty. It's vital that you understand every detail."

"Don't worry," Hassim interjected. "Any difficulty, I'll explain."

"Okay." Bolan reached into his holdall and removed an iPad. Left to his own devices, he much preferred a smartphone, as it was easier to carry and conceal, but he had known that at some point he would have to demonstrate to a larger group. Here was where the larger screen came in handy. Powering up, he brought up the intel that Kurtzman had sent him. A map appeared on the screen.

"You know, when Jared called me a pirate, he maybe wasn't too far from the truth." As he spoke, Bolan recalled the ironically sinking feeling when he had first read the emails forwarded by Brognola.

"Gentlemen," he said slowly. "Our objective is not actually in Latakia itself. It's moored half a klick out in the harbor..."

BOSNICH LOOKED OVER the yacht's stateroom once more. The main oval table was set with nameplates; the screen on the wall was linked to the laptop that lay idle to one side, on a smaller table from which the scientists would present and the auction would be conducted.

There would be twenty representatives in the room, bidding. Their entourages would remain on the boats that had brought them out into the bay. The rules had been set and agreed to, and the security that kept the merchandise contained would also form a ring of steel to ensure that this condition was not breached. Further to this, Singh had spent the morning in Latakia, speaking to the governor of the Latakia Muhafazah. Money had changed hands, and rather than hand over a sum and then hope that it filtered down as required, Singh had met with the members of the elected provincial council responsible for the manatiq and nahiya directly around the port and harbor area. From governor to region to district—every man who held a responsibility for that area had been primed to allow the meet to go ahead without interference.

Yet despite this, Bosnich felt a fluttering in his gut that was almost alien to him. A long time ago, he used to feel this before the commencement of a deal, but no longer. Yet why should this be different?

He knew why. Handling the merchandise was easy when

it was cold and inanimate. But this piece of merchandise was flesh and blood—it was prone to all the erratic nature of humanity.

This was the biggest deal that he and Singh had ever set up. It could not go wrong.

Assuring himself that the room was set, he left and strode down the corridors of the yacht until he reached the state-room where the two scientists were relaxing—if it could be called that. They looked as tense as they had earlier in the day. The presence of a guard in the corner was an undoubted spur to this. Ignoring his presence, Bosnich approached them.

"Gentlemen, are we set for tomorrow?"

Hoeness nodded shortly, but Gabriel was less assuring. "No. I fail to see why we could not have remained in our laboratory. There is still work to be done. If it comes to that, I do not see why we have to conduct this matter with such subterfuge. We are acting like criminals."

Bosnich held his temper as it boiled—the stupidity and arrogance of the man amazed him. How else did he think they could gain financing for such a project through unorthodox channels? Had he never wondered why two "entrepreneurs" with no relevant background would put up a sum that was hardly small change?

He forced a smile. "Europe is a territory in which many of those who wish to examine and bid for your knowledge would feel less than safe. A territory as neutral as possible, and that would attract as little attention as possible, is the only way to ensure that we get the funding we need. And that, after all, is what you wish, is it not?"

Gabriel grudgingly assented. "I suppose that is the case. I will be glad when this is completed and we can return to our work."

Bosnich detected the note of uncertainty and fear in the young scientist's tone.

"Do not worry," he assured him. "Nothing will disrupt the proceedings tomorrow."

"LET'S ROLL," HASSIM murmured, waving his hand to emphasize the words he would not risk at greater volume.

Bolan had to hand it to him—three jeeps acquired quickly, filled with necessary provision for travel and hardware, and twelve men rounded up, briefed, armed and ready to move in less than four hours. Hassim was earning the cash he would get at the end of this.

As the vehicles moved out into the night, along streets that were almost deserted, Bolan paused to consider what they were about to do. They would travel up to the border of Homs Muhafazah and from there they would take to the water. Bolan's initial thought had been to either take the road all the way around or find some way of crossing the water to Latakia, surveying the target along the way. Hassim had been unimpressed.

"The more we travel by road, the more we risk being stopped. You are lucky to catch a lull in the unrest. But it won't last long. Meanwhile, the lure of the shekel will ease our way only so far. It is unfortunate, but there are some soldiers who, amazingly, do not wish to supplement their incomes but in truth feel some kind of loyalty to their generals. The less chance we take of engaging with them the better. If we go by road as far as the border with Homs, we should be fine. I know the soldiers of this governance, and how susceptible they are. Under another rule I would not like to be so certain."

"What about boats?" Bolan had asked. "Surely any one place is as good as another?"

"In theory, perhaps, but local knowledge is what you pay me for, eh?"

With that, Bolan had been prepared to let Hassim take point for this part of the mission.

The three jeeps moved in convoy through the outskirts of the city until they hit a dirt road heading northwest. So far, they had seen little of the military presence that was supposed to keep the city in lockdown. When questioned, Hassim snorted and passed a comment on the government that had been less than complimentary, but had amused the other men in the jeep.

"The trouble with those dogs," one of the men had said in heavily accented English, "is that they want to keep the money to themselves. Look at us…all of us." A sweep of his arm took in himself and the two following vehicles. "Do we look like a people who have money from oil? Our land is some of the richest in this region, but do we look like we see any of it?"

"Same old story," Bolan said. "Not one that counts against an SMG, mortar or grenade."

"True. But like all of their type, the government and their army only go in hard when they know they can win… Look, this will prove it to you."

He indicated ahead. Coming toward them was an armored car, dusty and carrying two soldiers on the exterior, both with carbines held loosely.

Bolan looked back. The other two jeeps were behind them, but in the dark night there were no other indications of traffic or even habitation, the ribbons of light from their head-lamps being all that cut through the darkness.

The soldier was carrying a Tavor TAR-21 assault rifle. With a practiced and unconscious ease he brought it up so that it could easily be put in a firing position. He could feel the tension in the vehicle rack up a notch. Bolan didn't have to look back a second time to know that the same had happened in the two vehicles following.

The armored car approached, and the two men on the exterior snapped up from their previously relaxed postures. The armored vehicle slowed and started to turn so that it would cut across the road and block their way.

"Shadeeb, you know what to do," Hassim yelled over the noise of the desert wind and the roar of the engine as he held steady speed.

From a bag at his feet, the man who had spoken to Bolan with such contempt for the military opted to demonstrate this by producing an RPG-7 that he hoisted into position. With the armored vehicle presenting its side, and the two men on the exterior moving to adopt cover on the far side of the turret as the mounted gun swung around, it would seem that the military were, in truth, lining themselves up nicely for a broadside from the rocket-propelled grenade launcher that Shadeeb toted.

"Too easy," Bolan said to himself, at the same time hoping that the commotion would not draw too much attention. They seemed to be isolated out here, but the light and sound resulting from such a clash would all too easily alert anyone within several klicks of their position.

Shadeeb stood up in his seat as the jeep closed on the armored car, making sure that, although it exposed him as a target, the enemy could see his ordnance.

It was an extraordinary game of chicken, and Bolan marvelled at both the reckless bravado and utter stupidity of such a move.

All the more surprising then, when the armored car—at the behest of the gesticulating and shouting soldiers on the exterior—began to back up until it sat at the farthest edge of the road.

The three jeeps passed without reduction in speed and

without interference. In the reflected light of the headlamps, Bolan could see the men on the exterior of the vehicle glowering at the party as they passed, yet they made no move to intercept or pursue.

"You see?" Shadeeb said as the armored vehicle receded into the distance, placing the RPG-7 carefully back in the canvas bag at his feet. "They only have courage when they have the bigger numbers or the bigger guns." He spat out of the moving vehicle for emphasis.

"Let us hope we do not encounter any with more courage before the dawn," Hassim added. "We cannot afford the delay of a firefight if we are to make the bay by the time the sun rises."

"And then?" Bolan asked.

"And then we take a little boat trip." Hassim smiled. "Trust me, Matt Cooper. It's the only way to travel."

6

Dawn was breaking as they reached the coastal fishing village. With some outlying farms, and little sign of any military presence, it seemed to be a perfect launch point.

The jeeps drove up and stopped, creating a cloud of dust in the still morning air. Despite the early hour, there were people moving about, beginning their daily business.

"Wait here," Hassim told Bolan, before climbing down from the jeep and heading toward a small group of men clustered around boats that had been dragged from the water's edge to the shore. As Bolan watched, the group—he counted seven—turned to the approaching man. One of them said something that made the others laugh before stepping forward to accept the embrace Hassim offered him. Bolan was too far away to hear what was said, even assuming he could understand the dialect. He sat impassively, watching as some kind of negotiation took place.

The bay was wide, and even the most cursory glance showed that the far shore was not in plain sight. That would take them to the Muhafazah of Tartus—easy for him to remember as intel had told him that their target ship was called something not too far removed—and they would have to skirt the coast of this governance in order to reach their destination. Going by water would be easier than using roads—

faster, too. But the boats these men were clustered around didn't look like they could make the pace.

Hassim left the group and walked back to the jeep. "It's arranged," he said with a smile.

"I hope you're not expecting those vessels to make time," Bolan said, indicating the boats that the group still clustered around.

Hassim looked over his shoulder, then threw back his head and laughed aloud. "You think that I would? No, surely not." Then, likely noticing the soldier's set expression, changed. "Cooper, I haven't forgotten everything I learned over the years. Come with me."

Bolan walked in his wake as Hassim barked commands at his men. The jeeps roared to life and circled the edge of the village toward a stone-and-slate barn that looked disused.

"You know, Cooper, when you work for yourself you have to build a network of those you trust, and also a spread of equipment in places where it may be of use. This is such an instance. Behold."

Bolan had to smile—Hassim was enjoying this. And Bolan had to grant that it was worth savoring. His men poured out of their vehicles and opened the doors of the barn, revealing two powerboats on trailers. Both appeared to have been kept in good condition, and the men transferred the ordnance bags from the vehicles to the boats while moving the vehicles around to couple them to the trailers.

"We can make good speed with these." Hassim and Bolan watched the procedure. "Time will not be an issue. Watching for harbor and military patrols might. I do not suppose that with your intelligence sources you could determine points of caution?"

"It's asking a lot at such notice, but I can try." Bolan pulled the phone from his pocket and hit the speed dial to Stony Man Farm.

"Striker, nice to hear from you. Pleasant weather where you are?"

"You probably already know that, Bear. I need some intel and as fast as you can muster."

"I will always do my best by you, Striker."

"I'm standing in Rif Dimashq, on the border of Homs, and I'll be crossing the bay and circling Tartus toward Latakia. Obviously we would prefer not to engage with any harbor patrol or naval forces along the way. We don't have the time and we can't afford the attention."

"I'll get on to it. Harbor should be easy. Navy may take a little longer."

"Thanks. But try not to make it too much longer, Bear."

Bolan disconnected. Hassim nodded understanding and approval before indicating that they should join his men by the water's edge. The powerboats had been launched from the trailers and were in the shallows. The men had divided themselves into two parties and were settling into position. Men from the village dragged the trailers from the shallow waters and hooked them back up to the jeeps before removing them to cover.

"This is a tidy operation you've got," Bolan said as they waded out to join the boats. "If it stays like this, it should be a pleasure doing business with you."

"A PLEASURE DOING business with you," Vladimir muttered, palming a clip of cash into the hands of the harbor official. "You do realize the consequences of not carrying through your part of the bargain?"

The harbor official looked at the man standing before him—six feet plus of muscle and scar tissue, one eye clouded and the other boring into him with a cold ruthlessness. The official had six children and his salary was small. His wife was demanding. But he loved her and his children.

"I am aware. And scared, if I am honest."

Vladimir smiled, icy and vulpine. "Fear can be a good thing. You and your family will have a good long life if you listen to that voice well."

"I intend to."

The Russian nodded briefly, then left the harbor official's office and walked across the dock toward his vessel. It was painted in the colors of the Syrian naval forces, and to any onlookers the uniformed men on the deck appeared to be genuine. A gunboat with twin mounted cannon and machine guns, it was—to all intents and purposes—the real thing. The only indication that this was not the case became apparent when Vladimir came aboard without being challenged. He climbed to the bridge, where a small, squat man with a neck thicker than his skull stood waiting for him.

"Piotr, it is done," Vladimir said.

The squat man assented with satisfaction. "This is good. It should be a simple matter to resolve."

"I very much hope so. I prefer when things are smooth." He rubbed unconsciously at the scar that ran from below his ear under the collar of his black shirt. It was a remnant of when things had not run smoothly, and only Piotr's paramedic skills had prevented his demise.

The squat man turned to his comm system and gave the order for the gunboat to cast off. They would leave the harbor at Tartus and be at their destination in less than an hour.

"THREE HOURS AND then it will be under way," Singh said softly as he stared out from the bridge of the *Taurus*. He wiped his nose.

"I wish you would leave that until after the auction," Bosnich murmured.

"It keeps me sharp. We'll need that," Singh retorted. "With

merchandise like this, I will be very surprised if we don't have some kind of dispute during the day."

"There is nothing they can do on board," Bosnich said with a dismissive wave. "Negotiators and delegates, they pose no threat. All else is covered." He clapped Singh on the shoulder. "Just hold it together, my friend. This is going to be a great day… Why are you so quiet, now?"

Singh was staring out into the harbor. Coming in from the Mediterranean was a gunboat in Syrian colors. It seemed as though it was heading straight toward them. He frowned.

"What's that fucker doing? I laid out good money to avoid this."

"*We* laid out good money," Bosnich corrected gently. "Why worry? It's a long way off, and has plenty of time to change course…"

Spray from the warm Mediterranan cascaded over them as the prow of the powerboat cut through the water. Behind Bolan and Hassim, five men were hunkered down over the secured ordnance, grabbing what rest they could in the couple of hours it would take to make the distance. Already they were halfway there. The sun was presently high above them, moving across the cloudless sky, the heat becoming stronger.

Bolan checked his phone. No intel as yet. It wasn't like Kurtzman to have problems with something that was relatively straightforward.

In his mind, Bolan had the beginnings of a battle plan. They had two vessels. A pincer movement would divide the security on the yacht. Unless it was heavily armed, they would be up against men with handheld ordnance. What intel he had suggested that it was not large enough to carry any kind of heavy artillery. Reconnaissance would clear up this point. He checked his watch—if they kept on schedule, then there would be the time to do so. If current assumptions proved correct, their companion boat would draw fire and lay down cover while Bolan and Jared would lead the assault on the yacht. The aim was to board the vessel and take the two men who were their objective. Brognola had forwarded Hassim details on the men, including photographs, and he had made all his men aware of these during the briefing.

It wouldn't be easy, but it was a simple plan with little that could go wrong and push it off the map.

Looking to the horizon and then back toward the distant shoreline, Bolan was uneasy about the lack of vessels in the water—some fishing smacks at a distance, ignoring them, but that was all. While he welcomed the lack of interference, he would have expected to run into some routine patrols.

He hit the speed dial on his phone once again, yelling over the waves.

"Bear, talk to me."

"Strange days, my friend. There are usually patrols in the area both from provincial harbor authorities and from the military. But today there seems to be a distinct lack of activity, and in a very specific and localized area. I would suggest that your target has been at work with a touch of bribery. Good, in that it clears you a path, but bad—"

"In that they're very cautious. I'd expect nothing less, if I'm being honest. Thanks, Bear."

Bolan pocketed the smartphone and caught Hassim's quizzical glance, filling him in briefly on what he had been told.

"So, at least we know what to expect a little more than before," the grizzled warrior shrugged. "Your plan?" Bolan outlined his thoughts, and when he had finished, Hassim assented. "Seems reasonable."

The two men continued to stare ahead as the powerboats cut through the sea. There was nothing to do but wait. The entrance to the harbor at Latakia was finally within range of the naked eye.

Countdown began to tick in Bolan's mind.

"GET BELOW AND marshal the men," Piotr snapped. "We have less than five minutes before we are in range."

Vladimir immediately went below deck, barking orders as he did so. His assault team was already assembled, dressed in Syrian military uniforms and carrying weapons that were checked, locked and loaded. One of his team stepped forward at his command, handing him a spare uniform in which he dressed hurriedly. He knew that with his height and coloring he was an unlikely fit for an officer in the Syrian forces, but with good planning his enemy should not have time to assimilate this before being overrun.

Briefly, he recapped the maneuver for which they had been briefed. The enemy would not expect a Syrian vessel and would be momentarily disarmed. No doubt there would be an argument from one or both of the fools who presumed to set up the auction. This small amount of delay and confusion would be all they would need to open fire, and from there, locate target, secure and extract. It should take no more than a few minutes.

Vladimir felt the vessel move in the water, broadsiding as it came close to its objective. He indicated to his men to follow, and led them on deck.

As his head cleared the deck, he could hear the shouts of anger and confusion that were already emanating from the *Taurus*. His teeth bared in a grin as his feet hit the deck.

"WHAT THE FUCK is going on here?" Bosnich snarled as he picked up the walkie-talkie that connected him to his security chief. "Who are these jokers?"

He saw the security man turn and look in his direction as he spoke into his headset.

"They aren't responding to our shouts and they just keep coming. I thought the military were being kept out of this? I can't just order fire…"

"No, of course not. The last thing we want is an incident right now. Let them come alongside and allow the captain to board."

"Uh, looks like they want more than that," the security chief answered, his tone betraying uncertainty and nerves.

Bosnich didn't blame him. From below deck he could see a six-man team, led by an officer who didn't look, well, didn't look like an Arab to him.

"Hadji, I thought you'd—"

"I did, believe me," Singh said, his voice cracked with panic. "They must be from outside the region, but why—"

Bosnich snatched up the walkie-talkie again. "Those aren't military—that bastard leading them is no more an Arab than me. Chief, open fire and take protective measures. All men guard the merchandise." From under the bridge, he snatched up an HK-MP5, which he racked with the practiced ease of one familiar with arms. Adrenaline coursed through his veins and he felt alive. The nerves of the previous evening, when all had been peaceful, were paradoxically banished; at least this was something he understood. He turned to Singh, a wild grin slashing across his face. "You'd better get some firepower, Hadji. This is going to be short and ugly—like you, my friend."

As THE POWERBOATS entered the harbor, Bolan could see that something was seriously amiss. From the intel Kurtzman had passed on, he had expected to have a clear passage, but there was a gunboat alongside the *Taurus*—recognizable, as it was the only non-working vessel on the water—and even above the roar of the boat engines he could hear the crackle of gunfire.

"What the hell is going on?" Hassim yelled above the noise.

Bolan shook his head. "I don't know, but it looks like we might be too late for the party."

VLADIMIR HEARD THE security chief yell out to him, but ignored his words. He looked along the length of the yacht and noted the number and positions of the security men who were ranged along it. They were spaced evenly, and if his men were as accurate as their training suggested, this would be a simple task.

He barked orders at his men as they lined up, and from the corner of his eye noted the security chief's expression change as he recognized the language as Russian rather than Arabic. They were close enough for that, and he had little doubt that the chief noted his own wolfish smile.

But there was little time for such thoughts. His men, who had assumed a file like any military party, spread along the deck and racked their weapons, opening fire on the yacht before the security had a chance to react. Perhaps it would have been better to get aboard before the firefight began, but Vladimir figured that his appearance would blow that out at any closer range.

Even as this crossed his mind, he had leveled the M4 carbine that he favored, chopping out a short burst of 5.56 mm slugs that took out the security chief before he had a chance to return fire. The man had been distracted by his earpiece, and it had cost him—the precise reason why Vladimir avoided using such devices. Eliminating distractions kept you alive. As if to prove this, he skipped aside to avoid a burst of SMG fire that chewed the deck of the gunboat. It had come from the bridge of the yacht, and Valdimir made a mental note—the man firing would pay, if there was the opportunity.

Already, the gunboat was close enough to send across hooks and secure the two boats. The gap between them could be cleared with no problem and Vladimir took the lead, laying down covering fire as those security men who had not already been neutralized fell back to try and take cover. He fired a burst at the bridge, but there was no return; he guessed that whoever was up there had gone, possibly to secure the target.

The yacht was not built for paramilitary purposes—it was a leisure vessel primarily, and so was proving useless to the security forced back by the onslaught. Those who Valdimir's team had not eradicated had been forced to retreat below deck.

With a few yelled commands, Vladimir directed his men to scour the deck and bridge, securing the territory. Within a few moments, this had been achieved.

"How many exits?" he asked of his team.

"Three," the reply came. "One from bridge, two from deck. Bridge has been battened down. Two ways left in… or out."

Valdimir's face creased into a crooked grin. "Okay. Mask up, send down the CS. They make it too easy. Amateurs." He spat on the deck to emphasize his point before slipping on a gas mask, his men following suit. With pointing finger, he directed two men, to each lay down covering fire and lob a CS grenade into the interior of the yacht.

Chances were that these idiots did not have masks of their own. How they could have lucked into such a piece of property and hoped to bring off its sale was beyond him. They did not deserve such luck if they did not know how to take proper advantage. Still, they might surprise him and be in at least some manner prepared.

Thus it was that he counted off twenty seconds for the grenades' gas to start to spread before sending his men down in the formation specified before embarkation. He sent three men down one hatch and followed the other two down the one aft of the vessel. As the hatches sprang open, a mist of CS gas wafted up on to the deck.

As he descended the ladder leading below decks, the air from above caused the gas to dissipate quickly. Two three-shot bursts from the man at the front of the assault drew his attention to two of the security guards. Both had been disabled by the gas, with no masks, but had still attempted through streaming eyes and aching lungs to fire at the approaching party. Too slow. A tap from the lead man had taken each out in turn with a head shot.

Through the length of the boat Vladimir could hear yells and short bursts of fire, interspersed with longer bursts and the odd single shot. The latter two told him that some of the security either had masks or were made resilient through fear and adrenaline—his men would not waste ammunition on long bursts, nor risk a single shot.

But that was not his problem. For the moment, his job was to clear the below-deck areas and secure the targets. Obstacles were to be expected.

There were three doorways along the first corridor: two were open, and one was closed. Laying down cover, his men searched the open rooms. A tap through the lock of the third and the same procedure assured that this, too, was empty.

The gas was starting to clear, and as they progressed down a level it became obvious that the party entering from the fore hatch had made quick progress, as the dead bodies attested. It was only a few minutes before both parties linked up on the second level. Here, it was obvious that the last remaining security were making a stand as they held the assault party at bay.

Coming upon his men, Vladimir could tell at a glance that the remaining security were in one room. Sitting targets in one sense, but holding the ace nonetheless. Through his mask, he yelled at his men. "Pull back—they are expendable, but the targets must not be harmed."

His assault party included hired hands, local militia and guerrillas in search of funds, but they were well disciplined. They pulled back as far as possible.

Vladimir considered his options. The men inside must have masks, or had at least escaped the worst of the effects of the CS. He could not waste time in getting them out, and yet could not risk his targets being hit in any crossfire.

He reached across and tapped a grenade that one of his men carried on his belt. The man picked it off, looked at it and smiled behind his mask. He nodded and made to toss it across the divide and into the room where the targets were being held. As he did so, Vladimir indicated to his men to turn away and cover their ears.

It was unnecessary; they were already cognizant of his intention, and he joined them in facing away, covering his ears and closing his eyes while opening his mouth to create a hollow that would allow the concussion to pass without damage.

Even with their backs to the blast, they could see as well as feel and hear the concussion grenade, the flash lighting up the insides of their eyelids. In a couple of seconds it passed through them in the enclosed space.

Wasting no more time, Vladimir led his party into the room. There were three security men—identifiable by their similar clothing—lying disabled on the carpet and across the remnants of the long table, shattered by the blast. Each was taken out by a short tap from one of Valdimir's men.

At the end of the room, prone under a screen that had been ripped from the wall by the blast, were two armed men, and two unarmed men. The two unarmed men Vladimir could identify by sight as being the targets.

The two armed men—an Eastern European and an Indian—lay dazed and paralyzed by the effects of the blast.

So, the Russian thought, these are the amateurs who wanted to play with the big boys. It had been an ambitious, if stupid, effort on their part. He stepped across to them and lined up his M4 with the Indian's head. One short burst and the man was eliminated. He turned to the Eastern European and hesitated for a fraction of a second. The man, dazed and incapable as he was, tried to lift the SMG he held in his left hand, his eyes attempting to focus. Vladimir saluted his courage silently, but with one shot ended his resistance. Perhaps in another time and place, things would have been different.

Now there was business to attend to. He yelled through the mask and indicated to his men to take the remaining pair. Two to a man, they lifted them and carried them at the double as Vladimir took point with the remaining assault soldier covering their backs.

They took them up on deck and across to the gunboat; Vladimir ripped off his mask as he went. He could see Piotr on the bridge. He could also hear the approach of two motor vessels, at speed. He looked across and saw them coming from the open sea. Wondering who the hell they might be, but unwilling to take any chances, he ushered his men and their cargo across onto the gunboat, joining the crew in casting off and away from the yacht.

The engines of the gunboat came to life and it began to drift in the current, moving farther from the yacht and pointing toward the open sea.

With the approaching powerboats directly in its path.

7

"It's not going to get out of our way, and it's far better armed," Bolan yelled above the roaring whine of the engines and the crash of water against the hulls of the two powerboats as they came into alignment, running parallel as they entered the harbor and headed toward the yacht. Wisps of what could have been smoke or gas floated from the interior, and there was no sign of life since the raiding party had returned to the gunboat.

"Let them come." Hassim grinned. "They might have bigger guns, but we can move faster and split into two directions. Let them try and do that," he exclaimed triumphantly.

Bolan was less impressed with this notion than the leader of the men he had hired. It didn't matter if the two powerboats parted to draw fire to one while the other mounted an attack—he could see that they would possibly be outnumbered in terms of manpower, and could certainly be outgunned. The large cannon and machine gun that comprised the gunboat's firepower would chop them into pieces, and could certainly lay down enough covering fire to prevent their being able to do damage.

"We need to pull back, see where they head," Bolan stated.

Hassim looked at him as though he were insane. "You're scared, Cooper? Surely not?"

"It's not about that. We can't match their firepower and it

would be simple for them to pick us off one at a time. Better to circle and pursue, try to get them off the boat and on to neutral ground."

The mercenary leader made as if to reply, but events prevented his words of wisdom from being heard. Bucking over the tide of the harbor and the conflicting currents of the wash the two powerboats were effecting on each other, the boats were now within firing range of the gunboat as it turned and began to head toward the mouth of the harbor.

It was slower and more cumbersome than the other craft, but had brute strength to compensate. As the powerboats closed, the gunboat swung in one direction and its armaments swung around so that they were facing the oncoming powerboats. The waters were chopped up by spray as tracer shells from the machine gun spat into the waves, finding range.

Standing, Bolan swung an arm in the direction of the other boat, indicating a wide arc—he could only hope that the wordless order would be understood. The boat in which he stood took evasive action, swinging to proscribe its own wide arc around the path of the oncoming gunboat. The machine gun followed their path rather than that of the other powerboat, and Bolan ducked along with the rest of those aboard as fire from the gunboat shattered the windshield of the powerboat, showering them with glass and water as the waves swept in without opposition. It made it almost impossible for the pilot to see where the powerboat was headed and for Bolan to form any clear impression of where they were headed. The boat bucked and weaved in the waters as the pilot fought for control.

With that boat temporarily out of action, the gunboat swung its armaments around so that fire could be focused on the other boat.

Leaving them and not finishing the job was an error. As

the pilot wrestled his vessel back into some semblance of a course, Bolan barked at the men in the back of the boat to pass the RPG-7 that they had with them. Moving with the motion of the boat as best he could, thigh and calf muscles straining to keep him upright and balanced, he racked and loaded the launcher, balancing it so that he could sight the gunboat as his own vessel moved erratically in the waters. He loosed a load at the gunboat, the recoil making him stumble backward so that it was hard to see if the shot had any positive effect. Then, even over the whine of the protesting engine and the rumble of the waters, the explosion of the grenade was audible.

"Got the bastard," Hassim yelled, clapping Bolan on the shoulder as the soldier adjusted in order to get a clearer view.

A cry of victory, but a hollow one, as smoke and some fire on deck showed that the grenade had hit home, but the armor-plated deck was too solid and thick to really be damaged. It was superficial, but enough to distract the attention of the gunboat crew from the other boat. As the relatively slow and clumsy gunboat began to turn in the water, Bolan could see the other powerboat careening off across the harbor, the pilot seemingly struggling for control.

"Hardly scratched him, and now he's coming for us," Bolan snapped. "The other boat is out of their range, I suggest we do likewise."

"They will follow, and eventually they will catch us. We should stand and fight now," one of the men behind him yelled.

"They don't want to stay and fight, they just want us to leave them alone while they go," Bolan returned. "We can continue this when we have a chance to even the odds. Now get this toward port side, quick," he barked.

The pilot gunned his engine and took the vehicle around the still and silent yacht. Bolan could see that the other powerboat was doing the same. The gunboat fired a desultory blast at them, more to keep them on the run than with any hope of hitting them as they moved out of range.

As he had suspected—and hoped—the gunboat circled in the waters of the harbor, swinging around so that it faced toward the mouth of the harbor once more before gunning its engines to drive it out to sea at as great a speed as it could muster.

Bolan indicated to the pilot to take his vessel in alongside the yacht, trusting that the other powerboat, which seemed now to have come under control once more, would follow suit.

"Why are we looking there?" Hassim asked. "The quarry is long gone now." He pointed to where the gunboat was now exiting the harbor.

"We're looking for anything that might be useful—like anyone left still breathing," Bolan replied. "We need any intel we can gather."

DISORIENTED AND DISABLED as they may have been when they were dragged aboard, scientists Gabriel and Hoeness had soon recovered enough to be aware of what was happening to them. As the explosion of the grenade rocked the gunboat, and the chattering roar and booming of its own fire echoed below deck, they passed through fear, apprehension, and then anger and indignation. They were still feeling this as the firing died down, and the rocking of the boat as it bucked the waves set their stomachs churning.

Unsteadily, the younger scientist got to his feet and stumbled across the cabin in which they had been confined, trying the door and finding it secured. He shook his head at his companion and returned to his bunk, where he flopped down heavily.

Exhausted by their recent ordeal, both men lay silent for

some time, stirring only when the door to their cabin was unceremoniously thrown open and two armed men in Syrian uniforms stepped through, holding MP5s with which they covered the two scientists. Hoeness raised a weak grin; their assumption that either man may offer some resistance was absurd.

A third man stepped through the door. Tall, scarred and with an icy demeanor, his height and pale skin belied the uniform that he, too, wore.

"Gentlemen, I trust that you are unharmed," he said shortly.

"Apart from filling our lungs with gas and shooting at us, you mean?" Gabriel wheezed.

"Regrettable that you were involved, but also unavoidable—your previous owners were unwilling to give you up cheaply."

"Owners? You speak of us as though we are slaves."

The tall man shrugged. "Slaves. Merchandise. Saleable properties. It is all the same thing."

"Do you know who we actually are?" Gabriel's tone suggested that he was genuinely puzzled. "We are scientists. We were to meet representatives of many governments who were to bid for the rights to our research in return for funding further experiments. I fail to see what that has to do with the militia of the country in which the meeting is taking place," he added, indicating the uniform of those before him.

"It may have been relevant if one of the nations bidding at auction was Syria—which as far as I am aware was not the case—and indeed if we were of that country's military, which we are not. Gentlemen, I shall not prevaricate," he continued with the precise tones of one who is not speaking their native language. "You have been taken by a cartel that can see a great profit in selling your knowledge to the highest bidder. Of course, in order to do this, and to ensure completion of the research, then selling your knowledge entails selling your good selves."

"But that's ridiculous," Hoeness stammered, the crunching fear in his gut telling him that it was far from that.

The tall Russian seemed genuinely surprised by this. "But of course it does. That much must be evident. What do you think that the men we took you from were planning to do?" There was a moment's silence, and then the Russian continued. "Whatever you may have thought, there is no difference between what will happen to you now, and what would have happened if you had remained on the yacht. Perhaps, then, one difference—at least now you have been told honestly of your fate. Gentlemen, make yourselves comfortable. We will arrive at our destination soon, and you will then be informed of the next stage of this operation. You are not stupid men, so I feel I should not have to remind you, but..." He indicated the two men flanking the door, MP5s still leveled. "I suggest you resign yourselves to your fate and think about the personal terms you may be able to push for as part of a sale."

"You talk as though this were an ordinary business transaction," Gabriel spat.

A thin smile split the Russian's face. "All business comes down to the same. The people I work for have merely removed the false veneer of respectability."

Ushering out his guards and locking the cabin door behind him, he left the two scientists to ponder their fate.

"IN HERE," SHADEEB called from the stateroom of the *Taurus*. Bolan responded to the call, hurrying down the corridor. As he stood in the doorway, the faint smell of a charnel house mingled with the sharp remnants of the CS that clung to the air.

Shadeeb was standing at the far end of the room, between

the corpses of two men not in uniform. Bolan made his way across the room.

"Any ID?" he asked.

Shadeeb shook his head. "Not anything on them. They look like bosses, though. Manicured, and expensive clothes, even with blood and bullet holes. Maybe if we had time to search the boat properly—"

"We need to make this quick. Even if the whole region is turning a blind eye because of graft, a Syrian gunboat exchanging fire in the harbor is going to make someone nervous, no matter how much they've put in their safe. Doesn't matter who these guys were now, they're out of the game. It's who took the targets that matter."

"Then maybe this will help. Tell us something, for sure." Bolan grinned, bending down and picking up a shattered laptop from the floor. He ripped out the leads that had connected it to the screen that was broken and lying across one corpse. "Take it, Cooper. Screen is fucked, maybe the rest of its guts. But if the hard disk is okay—"

"Good thinking," Bolan agreed as he took it. "We can look at it at leisure. First we need to get the hell out, and quick."

Ushering Shadeeb from the stateroom, and with a last look around to see if there was anything else worth salvaging, Bolan moved through the lower level, calling to Hassim's men, urging them to move quickly. As he ascended the steps to the first level, he came across the mercenary leader.

"Anything?" Hassim asked.

"Your man found this, but that's it. No one left alive down there. Up here?"

"Nothing, and all dead. They were professional, whoever did this. We go now?"

"Sure as hell," Bolan said. The two men gathered their forces and took them up to the deck, where they rapidly descended into the two powerboats that had been grappled to the side of the yacht. Bolan stood on deck and made a quick survey of the area.

The waters were surprisingly calm. Those vessels that were on the move—mostly fishing vessels or small boats carrying cargo—were almost visibly avoiding the waters around the yacht. There was no doubt that all of them had been witness in part to the firefight that had taken place in the harbor, but they had noted one of the vessels to be military—and would have had no cause to doubt its authenticity—and in the country's current climate chose discretion.

As the powerboats turned and headed out toward the open sea, passing boats that steered clear from them, Bolan wondered how long it would be before the real military, and not an imposter, would take an interest.

"We'll head back toward the village," Hassim said briefly. "No point looking for them now. Besides, I don't know how much the boats could take," he added ruefully, as if noticing for the first time the damage that had been caused in the firefight.

Bolan was glad to hear it. He would not have to try and impose himself on the group. He didn't want to do this, and he had the feeling that he would need their manpower.

And soon.

"THAT'S NOT GOOD, Striker. It's not what I wanted to hear." Despite the words, Brognola's tone was more rueful than admonishing.

"Hal, it's not what I would have wanted to hear, either," Bolan returned. "It's not how I would have wanted it. There was no intel to suggest that there was an interested party who would want to muscle in."

"What have we got on them?"

Bolan laughed without humor. "I should be asking you that. They left nothing to clue us in and no one who could be questioned. They struck clean from their point, and they were efficient. Everyone on the opposing team was taken out. The only thing we could glean from the yacht was a shattered laptop. One of Hassim's boys is extracting the hard drive, and if it's in okay condition I'll upload the contents to Bear and see what he can make of it. At least then we'll know who was originally behind this, and maybe clean up the back end. But as for who took the targets…"

"Not military, that's for sure. They're trying to keep it quiet, but there's a lot going down. Heads will roll in that Muhafazah. There should be some nervous officials there tonight."

Bolan looked up to the cloudless, star-spangled sky. There would no doubt be fewer corrupt officials come sunrise, but that was of little concern or use to him at this time.

"It worked in our favor, too, so it's hard to criticize. I'd be more interested in anyone whose name comes up in connection with missing naval vessels. Though, we didn't board it, but we got close enough to at least say with certainty that it was genuine."

"I'll get Bear on to that."

"It's a good job the big man never sleeps. Your sources for the original emails—are they still an open channel?"

"Jumpy as a turkey the day before Thanksgiving, but they haven't got any choice but to be available."

"I won't ask. Keep them on red, Hal. I suspect that it won't be too long before they get mail from a new address, but with the same old offer. Until they do, we've got a cold trail."

Bolan disconnected with a sense of frustration. Recovering the laptop had seemed like some consolation, however small, but it could only yield information about the now-deceased parties. Where he went from here was still a blank wall.

"Hey, Cooper, you want to come look at this?"

Bolan turned to see one of Hassim's men walking toward him. He was a head shorter than the soldier, broader, and had a face that had spent too long under the desert sun. His name was Rafik, and he looked like he would cut you down if you looked at him in the wrong way. But despite his forbidding demeanor, there was a sparkle in his eye.

"Shadeeb got the hard disk extracted?"

Rafik nodded. "Got it wired up to his on an external. You want to have a look at what he's found before you upload it to your people?"

"Anything interesting?"

Rafik shrugged. "You tell us. Plenty on there, though."

He turned back toward the village, and Bolan fell in step with him. It was night, the villagers and the mercenaries were under cover, blankets draped over windows and doorways to cut down the ambient light. With the jeeps and now the powerboats secreted in barns, it looked like what it was most of the time—a fishing village that kept itself to itself. More than that, a village that liked it to stay that way.

In one of the buildings, Hassim and his men were gathered. Three women moved among them, distributing food, while they talked in low voices. Of the dozen men in the room, seven clustered around a rough wooden table where Hassim and Shadeeb pored over a laptop with an external drive unit.

"That interesting?" Bolan asked as he joined them.

"Listen, Cooper, we don't have satellite here, as the dish would attract too much attention, so any way that we can get our thrills. Have a look at this—I think you'll like it."

Shadeeb brought up the directory, and handed the laptop over to Bolan, watching what he was doing over his shoulder.

Bolan scanned the directory and then opened files as he methodically traced a path through the contents. This was not the time for him to look in any great depth, but he could see that there was much on here that would interest Kurtz-man, and not just because of the current mission. It became obvious that the main business of the men behind this operation was arms. There were detailed records of inventory, its storage and movement. Sales and records of delivery and payment, too. There would be a few regimes and organizations looking over their shoulders after Stony Man Farm received this intel.

Moving on, he found details of the laboratory that the deceased men had built for the target scientists, including location and financing. He would assume that the lab may still be open, not as yet closed and all evidence eradicated. If Kurtzman worked quickly, then Brognola might be able to glean some useful evidence and intel from the site.

Most important of all, stored on the disk was all correspondence from those who had been emailed concerning the auction, along with their various responses. It was as full a record as anyone could have hoped for, and this alone would be invaluable.

But there was even more than he could have hoped. In among the folders for the email there was one that did not belong to either a government, paramilitary or terrorist organization. An inquiry had been received from an organization that purported to be a trade alliance between corporations in the emergent East: the address and letterhead were likely to be false—but some of the names mentioned as being members and as those who had arranged contact between the vendor and this organization? These may just be for real. If so, then it could start the touch-paper on a trail that would lead Bolan to the organization that had engineered the day's coup.

"This is good...very good," he said softly. "I owe you, Shadeeb."

"I like your gratitude Mr. Cooper, but I'm a simple man. Cash would be preferable."

Bolan grinned. "It's worth a bonus." He pulled out his phone and hit the speed dial.

"Striker, not a good day so far, but Hal tells me you may have something for me."

"I just might," Bolan explained what he had found as he connected his phone to the laptop and sent the contents of the hard disk.

"Interesting," Kurtzman murmured as he perused the information on his screen. "It'll take me time to process all this, but I'll get us to work on the emails from the so-called trade alliance. I can't see any paramilitaries or nation states dirtying their hands before they've had a chance to make an open play. Too messy. But if these guys were rebuffed… how long do you have?"

"I couldn't say. Not long. Everyone who wanted to bid is in place in the region. My guess is that they have contact details, maybe by hacking the original vendor. They'll be in touch almost immediately, and they'll want to set it up somewhere in this region. It wouldn't make sense any other way."

"Right. But is Syria still a viable option?"

"You tell me for sure. I can't see it—it's going to be too hot. If they move down the coast, away from any concentration of NATO or UN forces, then first stop is Israel or Jordan. One would be a hell of a gamble, but the other? Bear, what's it like in Jordan right now?"

"Probably about as stable as anywhere in the Middle East—hell, more than most, I'd say. Not any direct coastal area, so less chance of it being a water-based meet, but maybe that was just a peccadillo of the late Bosnich and Singh? It's royal rather than republican, and has better stability and human rights than most of the region."

"Any meet there might attract attention without local unrest to hide behind, but that lack of trouble might make it easier to set up quickly. We're not going to move until I get word from Hal, but in the meantime send me as much detail about the region as you can—the usual, any geographic or topographic charts. Any friendly faces, too. If I can narrow down a few likely spots, then it might help when Hal gets word."

"I'll do that. Meantime, I'll keep on this and get back to you with anything I uncover that might help in some way."

"That's good. Gives me a warm feeling." He grinned.

"Hey, always happy to help."

Bolan disconnected the phone, and was lost in thought for a few moments. He was flying blind right now, but at least he might have some preparation in place when word came. He found it hard to believe that anyone setting up such an auction would be fool enough to try and step into the war zone that was Israel and Palestine. They wouldn't want to frighten away potential purchasers who had already had one unwanted and unexpected change of plan.

It was only when he became aware of the silence around him that he looked around to see that all eyes in the room were upon him, and he realized that—of course—they had been listening to his conversation.

Hassim raised an eyebrow.

"You want we should go to Jordan with you, Cooper?"

8

Gabriel had been silent and brooding for most of the short and uncomfortable trip. It had occurred to him that all had not been exactly as it seemed with Bosnich and Singh, and yet he had been driven by his desire to see the work that he and Hoeness had been undertaking at last receive recognition. He had put to the back of his mind the fact that no one gets something for nothing—there had to be a cost.

Then it hit him—he would not see his home or his family again. By entering into this Faustian pact he had separated himself from those he loved for all time. He wondered what had actually happened to the lab back in Switzerland. Had it been dismantled in order to be shipped to whoever bought their services? No, indeed, it was more like whoever had bought their *lives*. What would his family be told? Would they just be stranded, or would they, too, be packed up and shipped off to wherever the scientists were to end their days? At least that way he would see his beloved Elise again, it was worse for Hoeness, as the man had two children, one of whom no longer lived in the family home. What would that son be told?

Although the thought of their families being enslaved with them was appalling, the last option that came to mind was unthinkable. Yet there was no doubt that these were ruthless people. Gabriel looked across the cabin at Hoeness, who lay silent on his bunk. Was the same thing going through his mind, or did he blank it out rather than face the awful possibility?

They traveled in silence like this for some hours. Endless as they seemed in the pitch and yaw of the gunboat, it could not have been that long, as the effects of the CS gas were only just starting to clear from their bodies. Indeed, when the motion of the boat changed from a pitching roll to a simple up-and-down swell, Gabriel still found it hard to stand. His legs felt weak, likely to crumble beneath him.

Not that the men who came for them were in any way sympathetic. He could hear yelling from above and the pounding of feet outside in the corridor. The door was then flung open and two guards took up positions before the tall Russian—who, like the guards, was no longer wearing the Syrian uniform—entered.

"Gentlemen, can you walk?"

Gabriel came to his feet. "I can barely stand," he spat. "Whatever you expect from us, you will be disappointed."

Ignoring this, the Russian directed his next comment to Hoeness, who still lay on his bunk. "You—can you stand, or do you need assistance?"

"If it's assistance to get me home, then yes. Otherwise, go fuck yourself." His tone spoke of weary resignation to his fate rather than defiance, and Gabriel's blood boiled to see the Russian laugh.

"I like spirit. I do not ask idly, gentlemen. We are to transfer to another vessel, and if you are unable to walk, then we will assist you."

"You are too kind," Hoeness murmured.

The Russian smiled, his lips thin, twisted and chilling to view. "It is not kindness, as I am sure you know. My orders are to ensure safe delivery of the merchandise, and this I intend to do."

"In that case, as there is nothing we can do to stop you, you must render aid." Sarcasm dripped from Hoeness's words, and the Russian acknowledged this with another twist of his face, denoting amusement.

He signalled to men standing outside the cabin door. Four of them entered. Two assisted Hoeness down from his bunk and supported him out of the cabin and along the corridor. Gabriel did not need as much help, and was supported by one man while the other hovered around them.

Leading them up to the deck, the Russian had his men take them to the starboard bow. Despite the pitch and yaw felt below deck, the surface of the water seemed calm, and the Syrian gunboat sat easily in the water with another vessel—a yacht that made the *Taurus* seem like a life raft. It was sitting in the water a hundred yards from their vessel. A bosun's chair was slung between the two vessels in readiness.

Gabriel looked around as he was led toward it. There was no sign of land, and no sign of any other vessel anywhere on the horizon. It was as though they were the only two vessels on the ocean. Of course, he should expect nothing less as this had been a well-planned operation, and from the look of their intended berth was financed by parties with more backing than Bosnich and Singh could have dreamed of. Nonetheless, a part of him felt a pang of disappointment—and perhaps resignation—that there was no way they could be even accidentally overlooked.

The bosun's chair sat ready for him. He looked at the flimsy construction and then at the distance between the two vessels. The sea was calm, but even so...

"You're not serious," he said with a nervous cackle of fear. "I thought you were supposed to take care of the merchandise?"

"I'm glad you see it our way, even if it does take fear to bring you round," the Russian said softly. "You need not have that fear. This kind of lift has been used for hundreds of years. It is not as it looks."

He snapped his fingers, and before Gabriel had a chance to protest he was lifted and tied into the chair, which three men then proceeded to start across the watery divide, heaving on the pulley to propel the canvas chair and its valuable cargo across the space between the vessels.

Gabriel looked down and wished he hadn't—the calm sea did not look quite so gentle when you were swinging above it. The wine-dark depths and hard, glittering diamonds of light reflecting from the blazing sun seemed to threaten both to cut him and to envelop him. He felt his stomach heave and threw up into the water, splattering the surface.

Despite who they were, he had never been so glad as when he felt the hands of the men on the yacht deck take hold of him and unravel the knots that kept him secure. He had never been so glad to feel something solid beneath his feet. He could not look at the surrounding water, and kept his eyes firmly on the wooden decking as he heard them transfer Hoeness. In truth, such was the depth of his fear that he dared not look up until they had both been led below, into the relative safety of the yacht's interior.

When this had been done, the bosun's chair was dismantled. On the gunboat, it was gathered in and roughly stowed and secured where it could not float free on the surface and betray any position.

Up on the bridge, Vladimir joined Piotr. The fat man grunted.

"Did you see him puke? Pig. I ask you, if he cannot take what has happened to him so far, how will he and the other one be able to handle what will happen when they are sold? Hardware, not software, my friend. Our employers have not thought this through. What if these men cannot perform when they are sold?"

"There is no money-back guarantee, Piotr. And there does not need to be. We have completed our mission—"

"Not quite."

Vladimir shrugged. "Very well, but we have completed the most difficult part."

"What about those powerboats? Who sent them?"

"Does it matter now? We were successful, they were not. And they have not tracked us. More, it will be impossible for them to pick up a trail that lies at the bottom of the sea. All we have to do is to keep a secure ring around those two until the sale is complete, then collect our pay. The rest is not our concern."

"I hope you are right," the fat man mused. He looked out to where the yacht was already receding into the distance, headed for land. "How long should we give them?"

Valdimir clapped him on the shoulder. "You are nervous, Piotr. Do not be."

The fat man grunted again. "I prefer *cautious,*" he said dourly.

"Very well. We set the charges for forty-five minutes. They will be well on their way by then, and with our small boats we can catch them easily before we come too close to shore."

"Then do it," Piotr assented. "I will give the order for disembarkation."

Leaving his opposite number to complete his part of the task, Vladimir descended into the bowels of the gunboat. It seemed a shame to dispose of it in such a manner, as it had cost them a lot of their resource allocation, and to have a fully equipped gunboat could prove to be handy in the future. Of course, docking it may prove a problem, but…

He realized he was allowing his mind to race away from the matter at hand. As he reached the engine room, he heard Piotr's voice over the in-ship comm system issue the order for all personnel to assemble at the emergency boat points, ready to abandon ship.

As he prepared the charges and made his way from one end of the ship to the other, placing four charges along the way in areas where they would cause stress fractures in the hull and so directly allow flooding in the least amount of time, he mused on how disciplined his crew was. They shut down systems and gathered their belongings with a minimum of fuss before proceeding to the embarkation points. Not bad for what had a short while before been a rag-tag assortment of mercenaries and paramilitaries who had never worked together before, and rarely individually under the kind of discipline insisted upon by himself and Piotr.

By the time he had laid the last charge and was making his way back up to the deck, the gunboat was deserted. Once on deck, he found that one of the motorized dinghies had already been launched and was turning to head in the direction taken by the yacht. The other was descending into the water, and was followed by the remnants of the crew as he and Piotr made one last scan of the deck.

"Ready?" the fat man asked.

Vladimir nodded. "When they go, the chain will spark the ordnance aboard. She will already be shipping water. Down one way and out the other. There should be little left to see."

"I would prefer nothing. Not even a slick of oil or fuel."

"I can guarantee much, but not that. Unless anything works loose, there will be no objects to identify her."

Piotr sniffed. "Very well. It is the best we can hope for, I suppose."

Vladimir laughed. "You are a miserable bastard, Piotr Ilyich."

For once, a smile cracked the man's fat face. "That is why I am still alive, and don't you forget it."

With which he clambered down the rope to the dinghy

in ungainly fashion, followed in short and smooth order by his gaunt partner.

The dinghy pulled away, its motor straining as it set off in pursuit of its companion. There was silence in the boat, and the two Russians did not break this, even when, after the time had elapsed, there was a distant and hollow explosion far to their stern, followed by a series of smaller, subsidiary explosions.

They did not look back, though Vladimir did break the silence.

"It is a pity. It would have been useful to have our own gunboat."

BOLAN LOOKED HASSIM squarely in the eye. "How much would it cost?"

"More than you could probably muster in the necessary time. It's not that we wouldn't come. You think we wouldn't like a crack at the bastards on that gunboat?" He gestured to encompass the others in the room. Bolan took them in. To a man there was a muttering of consent that showed there was the element of the personal about this—whether or not that was a good thing was another matter.

"But there's something else, right?"

"Right," Hassim affirmed. "If they are headed for Jordan, then they're on safer ground than if they messed with the Israelis or screwed around on the West Bank. Those evil scum would take them out just for the hell of it. But Jordan? They have no ax to grind, no real problems right now. Except one."

"Palestine," Bolan nodded. "They were being overrun with refugees and exiles."

"Right. So they started this yellow card shit. If you're Palestinian and live in Jordan but have family on the West Bank, then you can go back and forth. If you don't, you're fucked. I think…if you live on the Gaza Strip then you ain't getting into Jordan even if you claim the king is your third cousin twice removed. They're tight. They don't want nothing to do with the Gaza Strip as they spent over twenty years fighting the Israelis. That was another twenty years back now, but they've got long memories."

"You figure I've got a better chance of getting in on my own than I have with you?"

Hassim laughed. "We're Arabs, Cooper. So are they. And they're going to take a long hard look at us. But you? You're a white guy, you can be anything it says on any of your passports and move around a whole lot easier."

"Fair point," Bolan conceded. "Leaves me light, though. I could use backup."

"And we'd gladly do it for the money and the fun of it. But we can't use water as there's no real way we could land without scrutiny. No coast, and what there is on the West Bank—our only way in—gets looked at closely. By road, it'd take us one hell of a journey, and it would be almost impossible to get across any passable roads because of checkpoints."

Bolan considered this. Solo he would be more flexible, could move quicker. Air would be fast, but he would have to leave ordnance behind, with no guarantee that there was a supply source at the other end. Road, maybe. On his own, that was possible, but it still left him with the knowledge that he would be up against a sizeable force with no backup, assuming there were no friendly faces in Kurtzman's contact book.

What the hell—he'd faced worse.

"It'll just have to be that way, then," he said.

Hassim laughed. "You got balls, Cooper. Let's hope you get to keep them. Pity those bastards aren't headed for Egypt. We could arrange a little boat trip for that one. Places to land aren't so hard to find as places to park, you know?"

"You might get your chance," Bolan mused. "Until I hear, Jordan is just the most likely location. In which case…"

Excusing himself for a moment, he retrieved his handgrip from where it had been stowed with the duffel bags containing his ordnance. When he returned, he could see that Hassim's men were seated around the tables, talking loudly and excitedly, too fast for his basic Arabic to grasp in full. What he could understand told him that they were discussing the best routes for him to cross into Jordan without running the risk of being detained.

There were twelve of them, along with Hassim, in the room. Rafik and Shadeeb he already knew. The other ten were a jumble of names and faces to him. There had been no real time to assimilate them, but he knew that Hassim trusted the group, and that was enough. Looking at them, they were a mixed bunch of men—some little more than boys, like the one he had first encountered in Hassim's store, while others showed the scars of war and the wear of long years toiling on the land and against an enemy.

Most of them were rangy and tall, lean with muscle and the hardships they had endured: Aref, who was an old friend of Hassim's, Haithem, who had just one eye, the other now a wound bound by scar tissue; Riad and Kamal, who were brothers; and Adib, who was the most silent, yet had the brooding air of someone about to explode with anger. Then there were the younger ones: Sami and Husni, both of whom looked too soft to fight, being chunky and well-fed; Gamal, the boy Bolan had encountered in the store, and who still looked at him with a glimmer of suspicion; and Abd and Amin, who were rangy youths resembling nothing so much as the sons of the older, more experienced fighters, even though they were not. A mixed band of age and ability, perhaps, but bound together by camaraderie with their brothers—something that Bolan knew, better than anyone, could overcome disadvantages.

He would be sorry if he had to leave them behind, and perhaps for more reasons than just having to fly solo. But there would be time to worry about that later. For the moment, he could use the help they seemed willing to offer.

Bolan stepped into their midst and took the iPad from his handgrip, powering it up before calling up the charts that Kurtzman had downloaded for him. Although he had kept his Arabic to a minimum, preferring to be translated via Hassim and avoid misunderstandings, he paid them the courtesy of addressing them in their own language.

"Gentlemen, if I am to journey into Jordan on my own, I would appreciate your guidance. I have some maps, but they are no substitute for the knowledge of experience. If you would look at them and advise me…"

He grinned as the whole room seemed to converge on him, arguments and jabbing fingers already indicating points of contention.

DAWN WAS BREAKING as Bolan stepped outside to take the incoming call from Stony Man. Behind him, the group of mercenaries lay across the tables and floor of the building. They had argued and planned for hours, to the extent that Bolan now felt as though he had an intimate knowledge of the region. He was also pretty sure, from what he had been told, of the likeliest region of the country in which any quick auction could be arranged.

"Bear, speak to me."

"You sound wide-awake considering it must be early morning where you are," Kurtzman said wryly.

"I'll snatch a couple of hours shortly. I've just been through the kind of briefing that you could only imagine," Bolan replied with a grin.

"I'll take your word for it. Good news and bad news, Striker."

"Bad first, then," Bolan replied, killing the grin.

"Two sides of the coin, there, so I'll just lay it straight. I think we've nailed who they are, and they've not wasted any time in setting up a new meet. Jordan, as you suspected. They must have headed straight there when they took the targets, and had an auction site set and ready to go."

"That's fine. I was pretty sure it would have to be there, so I've been planning accordingly. I've got a route and transport lined up, and I figure I can get in with ordnance. Can't take any backup though, so I'm relying on you to give me a name."

"That's the flipside of it, Striker. We have no one in the area that we can hook you up with—for backup or supply. So just as well you can supply your own. It's been quiet there of late, and the people we did have are either inactive or moved on. It's going to have to be a solo op."

Bolan sighed. "I was really hoping not to hear that, Bear. And I'm thinking, from the tone of your voice, that's not the only downside."

"The auction is twenty hours away. If you go by road then you're at least sixteen hours away."

Bolan cursed. "Doesn't give me a lot of time to reconnoiter. They've emailed location and maps, right?"

"That's the one good thing. They've had to forego certain precautions in order to set this up so quick, and that's given us an advantage, thanks to Hal's mole."

"Send me everything. I'll be setting off immediately and will do some studying on the way."

"I hope you've got a good driver, Striker."

Bolan looked back to the building where his erstwhile compatriots rested.

"Right here and now? The best, Bear."

9

Twelve hours in, Bolan lay across the back of the jeep, trying to get some rest. There was a lot to think about, but he
was long practiced in the art of switching off—the problems
would still be there when he awoke, and he would be in a
much fresher frame of mind. That wasn't the issue—it was
these damn roads and the desert that were causing him grief.

A simple plan: two jeeps, one with Hassim and Bolan, the
other with Rafik driving and Gamal riding shotgun. Hassim would take the wheel of their vehicle, allowing Bolan
to get some rest as they made their way to the small line of
border that lay between Syria and Jordan that would put
him in direct line for his target destination. When they were
within twenty klicks, Bolan would take the wheel and proceed across the border alone to his destination. Hassim would
wait with the others, making camp. They would wait thirty-
six hours. If Bolan returned, Hassim would drive him back
to the village, allowing him to rest. If he did not return, they
would mourn the loss of their vehicle and travel back alone.

Twenty klicks was far enough back that the border patrols
would not stumble on them. Thirty-six hours would allow
Bolan to get to his destination, effect his mission and then
return. Anything else allowed too much margin of error.

The plan would have been great, if not for the fact that the
roads were in poor condition and they needed to go off-road

for great swaths of territory. The land was dry scrub, desert in places, with rocks treacherously hidden by the thin, sandy soil. It was not a smooth ride, and although Bolan was used to snatching z's in the most unlikely of places, the constant jarring was proving to make his rest fitful, at best.

It would have been easier if he could have flown via Jack Grimaldi and Dragonslayer, but local conditions made this impossible. As part of the sanctions the Arab League had imposed when Libya was going down, there had been an exclusion policy and a no-fly zone over much of Libya and the surrounding territories. Even the UN planes that had been part of taking down Gaddafi had encountered problems. Although the despot had joined the league of great dictators in the even greater beyond, the fragile state of the National Transitional Council had made the other states in the region nervous, neighboring Egypt in particular. So the Arab League had kept no-fly in place: scheduled commercial flights and a state airforce were fine. But anything that didn't fit this profile was a no-no. And as Syria was in a delicate political position and was not, unlike its neighbor Jordan, a part of the Arab League, having been sanctioned and excluded, anything that took to the air from there and wasn't immediately accountable ran huge risks.

It would take a lot to shoot a flyer like Grimaldi and a chopper like Dragonslayer out of the sky. But worse than that would be the possibility that they were in some way tagged and traced back to the homeland. Questions would be raised that no one would want to answer.

So Bolan found himself relying on water transport and four wheels. Not the most comforting thought that went through his mind as he drifted in and out of sleep during the journey.

He was finally jolted awake by the grinding of gears and the sudden shunt of the jeep pulling up. Hassim leaned over and whispered in a hoarse voice, "Hey, Cooper, wakey wakey. We're here…"

"I kind of gathered that," Bolan said as he stood and stretched. He got out of the vehicle and looked around. The other jeep had stopped about ten yards away, Rafik and Gamal staring at him. Bolan got out his smartphone and used the GPS to locate himself in relation both to the border and to his target destination.

"Border's that way," Hassim said, waving a hand unnecessarily in the direction the jeep was facing.

"Thanks, I'll bear that in mind," Bolan said wryly.

"Yeah, funny man," Hassim replied. "Listen, there's not much land on the border between us and Jordan that causes problems. Most of it has been pretty easy for tribal movement over the centuries. But just lately, the way things are… some sections get patrolled a lot heavier than other stretches."

"Frequency? What kind of patrols?" Bolan asked, needing some kind of specific.

"Every few hours around here. You just drew the short straw is all. It had been more, but things have been quiet of late, so they've slackened the pace. Usually a jeep with a mounted gun, sometimes an armored car. Three, four men tops."

"What will they do when they see me coming?"

"If they do—and you go carefully, you should avoid that— then they'll want papers. You're American, so pretend you're some fuckwit Fox newsman who's got himself lost."

"I think I can manage that," Bolan said, amused.

"Yeah, well you won't get the kind of interrogation we get. You got the hardware secured?"

Bolan nodded. His duffel bags were stowed in sections of the jeep that had been cut away to provide compartments for concealment. It would take a thorough search to find them, let alone work out how to access them without prior knowledge.

"Then all I can do now is wish you well, Cooper. We'll wait and pray. May your God go with you."

Bolan acknowledged the touch of the forehead from Hassim, and climbed into the jeep. Laying the smartphone on the seat beside him to act as a compass, he put the jeep in gear and left the other vehicle in his wake. He did not look back, but if he had, he would have seen that Hassim stood watching for some while, a thoughtful expression on his face.

"Crazy bastard," Hassim murmured softly. "No wonder I never went back..."

BOLAN PUSHED THE engine to its limit. Looking at the time, he could see that Hassim had made good progress to get them close to the border quicker than had been estimated. But he would still be cutting it fine.

By the GPS and the jeep's own distance indicator, he should be hitting Jordan any minute. He had cut across scrub from his starting point and had taken to the roadway as soon as he could. He figured he was running parallel to the border at present, and the curve of the road would take him over shortly. There was no sign of any border guards or patrol, either before or behind him. With luck, he would get into the country unimpeded. But even if this was the case, he still had a hell of a journey.

The West Bank was the big problem: in order to avoid the issues that arose when trying to cross there, they had been forced to travel out of their way until they passed the Governorate of Irbid and had reached the border of the much larger, but less important Mafraq. Over twenty-six thousand klicks square, it was by far the biggest single expanse of land in Jordan, and also the most sparsely populated. Irbid was one twenty-fifth the size, yet had four times the number of peo-

ple squashed into it. This was partly because it was close to
Jordan and also bordered Israel and the West Bank. Trade,
merchant links, and the fact that it was about as near as any
Jordanian could get to the sea accounted for much. But it
also had a lot to do with terrain. Bolan was presently, by his
reckoning, in Jordan, and heading west. Doubling back on
himself, in a sense. If he could have crossed straight, it would
have saved him time. At least he wasn't headed east. The
land he currently drove across was dry and sandy—farther
east and he would have been traveling on the plateau that the
country mostly stood upon. Hot, arid desert land that was
unwelcoming. At least, as he headed toward Irbid, he was
moving into the more mountainous and hilly region of the
Jordan valley, where the climate was a little more temperate
and the land less forbidding.

But not entirely. As he kept the jeep steady on the slowly
unwinding, empty road, he referred to the material Kurtzman had forwarded to him.

The auction was to be held in Ar Ramtha, which was the
first section of Irbid that he would hit. It was an indepen-
dent section of the governorate that had devolved a degree
of its own administration. From what he knew of Jordan,
he figured that despite this, it would be no easy task for the
cartel staging the auction to quiet the locals in the same
way that their predecessors had managed in Syria. Jordan
had less corruption, less unrest, and was generally a more
settled territory.

So, why there? What had made it an ideal place?

According to the maps that Kurtzman had sent him, the
auction was to be held on the edge of an area of irrigated
land that had been part of an agricultural development area.
During the upheavals of the previous year, the project had
fallen prey to neglect, and the farmers in that area had deserted it in droves.

So it had good communication with the cities and was also relatively empty. It was therefore easy to get to and unlikely to be overlooked, with no major center of population to disturb the business at hand.

Even though it was as close to the edge of Irbid as it was possible to get, it was still too close to the densely populated regions for comfort. It smacked of a compromise between the need for security and the need to get the bidders in place quickly.

That should suit him fine.

When he came to the first empty dwelling, he pulled the jeep off the road and parked where he could cover the vehicle. He took the duffel bags from their hiding place and checked that he had enough water and provisions to keep him afloat. Looking at the time, he had five hours before the auction was scheduled to take place. Using the GPS on his smartphone and taking account of the details sent by Kurtzman, he figured that if he took a course bearing north by northeast, then he would be able to circle the auction location.

He walked at a steady pace, keeping up his speed. It was odd to be hiking through a territory that should be busy with farmers gathering in a citrus fruit harvest. The trees were a strange combination of the withered and those that could still take moisture from the ground and were bearing a strong crop. That these were few and far between spoke volumes of the irrigation problems. He paused to take an orange, eating it as he progressed through deserted groves.

After three-quarters of an hour, the groves began to thin out even more and he was in a territory that had been deserted for longer; the land was more sparse scrub than anything else, and even empty dwellings became thin on the ground. As he moved, keeping one eye on his GPS, he noted that this was a flat land that would make it hard to find cover. The closer he got to the target area, the more he would have to keep low. There was nothing in the sky, and given the no-fly zone he was pretty sure that he would not be spotted by from above.

Three klicks, according to the information he had been given. The auction site should be dead ahead. He came up over a rise, careful to keep himself low to the ground. He scanned for motion detectors and cameras: there were none that his limited tech could pick out. He would have to rely on sight and instinct to carry him on—but at least he had field glasses.

It was an interesting conceit. A limo, two Humvees and a trailer were gathered around a Bedouin tent that was likely to serve as the auction room. There were four security men in view, though he knew there must be more. Despite the fact that they were in a deserted area and the auction was not due for a few hours, they looked on full alert. There was little sign of life, though he could not see inside the tent.

The trailer, like the kind used on movie locations, was large enough to keep three or four people comfortable while still being easily transportable. If his target bodies were anywhere, they were there.

Keeping his distance and a low profile, he circled the encampment. A 360-degree orbit revealed that there was no real cover for him at any point—which meant that the site was left exposed, too. But this was a minor consideration, as the security could be prepared before any large forces— easily visible—came within range.

It was as good a location as could have been selected in the time available. And he was certain that they had been pressed for time. There was no indication of any motion sensors or cameras at any point in the circuit he had proscribed. Something that suited him fine, as he had stopped at evenly spaced points along his circuit, planting small charges of C-4 and Semtex, timed to go off in an irregular pattern and at irregularly spaced, albeit close, intervals. He had been careful to use only a little of the explosive for each plant—it wouldn't pay to waste his resources. There was no chance of the charges doing any damage at that distance, but they would create the impression that there was more than just the one of him, and by their irregular nature cause some confusion about the direction of any assault.

Having come full circle, he settled back into position. Tracking the guards with his field glasses, he worked out that they moved in two patterns, each overlapping, and in opposite directions so that there was no section of the circumference that couldn't, at any point, be covered with ease by the defending forces.

They were good—or, at least, whoever drilled them was good.

He checked the time: two hours until the auction. He figured that the bidding parties would not risk arrival until just before time. Could he bank on that, though? Best not to, which was why he had set the charges to begin going off in the next fifteen minutes.

He prepared himself for the attack. The HK G3A4 with collapsible stock and 20-round mag would be the best choice under the circumstances; he also made sure that he carried shrapnel, CS and concussion grenades. He had a Glock 23 semi-automatic pistol, which would be a useful backup should the HK go down. He didn't want to go in with too much ordnance to slow him down.

Get in, cause chaos, locate and secure the targets, and use one of their own vehicles to effect a getaway while disabling the others. Hardly a detailed battle plan, but given the time and resources it would suffice.

10

"My friend, we are set?"

Piotr leaned over the table in the trailer. Although he spoke to the man behind him, his bulging eyes, cold and watery, were fixed on the two men who sat before him. Hoeness and Gabriel were bowed and ragged, aching and miserable. Neither man knew what to expect from the future, though both had dark suspicions. They could not look at the Russian. There was a moment of uncomfortable silence, punctuated only by the rattle and hum of the trailer's air conditioner.

The silence was eventually broken by the laconic tones of Piotr's tall, scarred compatriot, who stood in the doorway of the trailer, eyeing the two scientists with a wry contempt.

"The business room is laid out, and the area has been secured. Our men now patrol as proscribed."

"Your English is progressing strongly, my friend. Would that I had your grasp of the language." Despite the words, there was no humor in his voice. He continued, "But perhaps I would be better speaking in German? A language I believe we all understand and speak to a greater degree?" He switched languages midspeech, and could see immediately that the two scientists understood him more easily. He, too, felt more comfortable. "Right, you two pieces of shit. I can speak plainly and to the point. You are here, and you will be sold. I look at you now and you are crap. Who would believe that you have the ability to unlock secrets that are worth millions of dollars? You look like shit and you are sitting like you are morons. Who would buy you?"

"Can you blame us?" Hoeness muttered, with all the resistance he could muster.

Piotr reached out and hit him hard across the face with an open palm. "Shut up, you shit. We have been paid a lot of cash to bring you here and oversee the auction. We have to get a good price for you, or else we will suffer. And if no one wants you because they think your product is shit, then you will know what pain is. No easy end for you, my friend. If you want to live, then you sharpen up. If we suffer, you will suffer first. Understand?"

He stared intently at the two men, who shuffled fearfully in their seats before grunting a mild assent.

"Good," Piotr nodded. "This trailer has a shower unit—use it. There are clothes in the cupboard that should fit and are clean. Wear them. And sharpen up. Now!" He turned away toward the door and his partner, whose mouth quirked into a savage grin.

"You always were a motivator of men, Piotr."

Piotr spat on the floor of the trailer. "Men? Don't make me laugh," he snarled in Russian. "I will be glad when this is done. We are soldiers, not fucking used car salesmen. This part of the mission should have been down to others. We should just deliver."

Vladimir shrugged. "Time is tight, my friend. What is that stupid English saying? 'Needs must when the devil commands'? Something like that."

Piotr looked at him strangely. "What the fuck are you talking about?"

"Thinking on our feet, Piotr. That is what our paymasters are doing, and what they require of us. I am no more comfortable with this than you, but as we move so quickly, then who would be able to catch up with us before our mission is complete?"

Piotr did not answer immediately. He looked out of the door of the trailer at the desert and scrub that extended as far as he could see, and at the men they had hired on recommendation, so far performing more than adequately.

"Who indeed?" he murmured. And yet there was still that uneasy feeling in his gut that they were out of their usual territory—something that made Piotr nervous.

It was then that the silence of the desert was ruptured by an explosion.

BOLAN CROUCHED DOWN and watched intently, not flinching as the blast went off forty-five degrees to his right. His attention was focused entirely on the encampment.

Although it was too far away to actually be an attack on the camp itself, its shock factor caused the kind of confusion he wanted. He saw the open door of the trailer, and the fat man and the tall one he recognized from the deck of the gunboat conversing before the explosion attracted their attention. He saw the guards suddenly interrupt the patterns they had been making. As he'd surmised, they were going through the motions, but had not been expecting an attack. Complacency was a bigger threat than a man with a gun sometimes.

They broke their formation and began to rush toward the area of the explosion. He could see the two Russians—who from his intel, he had little doubt were ex-KGB or OGPU men gone freelance—yelling and trying to establish control and some kind of order.

He couldn't let that happen—time to mix it up a little more. He triggered an explosion that was just a little less than 180 degrees opposite.

The reaction was immediate. Half of the men changed direction, partly from reaction to the blast and partly because of the yelled orders they received. As the complete force seemed to have congregated at the sounds of the blast, Bolan had them all within a narrow band of range.

There was no way that he could take them all out, but he could certainly even the odds. Sighting, he tapped off four short bursts. In the ensuing confusion, only three of them hit—two men dropped, one with his face blown away and the other losing half the side of his head. A third guard was wounded but by the way he spun as he fell, it was clear that he was still alive, albeit incapacitated.

Having given away his own position and attracted some return fire, he needed to move. He triggered an explosion that was only fifty yards away from him in order to throw up a cloud, deflect his opponents' aim and provide cover to move. Where fire had pitted the sands around Bolan, forcing him low, it now moved to his left, enabling him to crawl at double speed in the opposite direction. As he moved farther from the field of fire, he straightened a little and broke into a run, triggering another explosion that would take the opposition fire away from him.

Relocating, Bolan took aim and fired another three short bursts into the rapidly dispersing opposition forces. This time he only took out one man, caught in the back of the head as he turned to try and follow the direction of the blasts.

As he circled before the return fire could pick out his location, Bolan wondered how he would progress from here. He could try and pick them off, but he was running short of charges to distract them. Come to that, the Russians were smart even if their troops were not, and would soon catch on...if they hadn't already.

IN THE TRAILER, Hoeness had been moving toward the shower unit in a despondent fashion when the first explosion sounded. He screamed and hunkered down on the floor.

Gabriel went rigid with fear. After what had happened to them in the past thirty-six hours, both men were stretched to the edge of sanity. They were used to the quiet of the laboratory—this was not what they had foreseen in any way.

But there is a stronger instinct than fear in most men—that of self-preservation. While Hoeness screamed, almost fetal on the floor, Gabriel felt a wave of calm sweep over him. He knew that if they stayed like this, they were certainly dead. To keep alive meant to keep hope. They were sitting ducks in the trailer—and Gabriel had little doubt after recent events that they were the target of this attack. They had to move.

With a slowness and care that didn't truly reflect the way that his mind raced, he rose to his feet and went over to Hoeness, gently lifting the man up. Hoeness was still screaming. Gabriel hit him, hard, across the face. The older man suddenly stopped screaming and looked at him with an expression of complete bewilderment. It sort of felt good—Gabriel felt in control of something, and God only knew that this was a rare feeling of late.

"Tomas, what the hell is happening?" the older man asked softly.

"More of these fucking lunatics wanting to take us," Gabriel replied flatly. "We should never have gotten into this, but it's too late now to worry about that. We need to make sure we are safe. Maybe we can even escape." He paused, waiting for an answer. He was rewarded by a look of hopelessness.

"No…how? Where are we, even?"

"Who knows? Who the fuck even cares? I know it's desert, but in which one of these godforsaken Arab lands is beyond me. All I know is that if we hang around, then all that's going to happen is that we'll keep getting this shit and sooner or later we're going to die. If we can make a break, then at least we have a chance."

Hoeness was apparently not convinced—perhaps he saw it was just another way to die.

"Okay. What do we do?" the older man said, with more than a little hesitation.

"I'm fucked if I know. Just play it by ear and try and find a jeep, then drive and hope for the best."

"That's a plan? Hardly scientific."

"These are hardly lab conditions. Now shut up and follow me," Gabriel snapped in reply, heading for the door.

He looked out at the confusion: shouting and gunfire. Only a hundred yards from the trailer he saw the two corpses of the guards who'd been shot, their heads almost unrecognizable, bleeding into the sand and already attracting flies as men hurried around them, ignoring what was at their feet.

Gabriel felt his stomach churn, but he fought and bit back the bile. Tearing his eyes away, he could see a jeep standing at the edge of the encampment, miraculously isolated from the activity around as the guards' attention was distracted in another direction.

Gabriel pulled Hoeness out of the trailer and toward the jeep. The older man staggered at his heels. Gabriel clambered into the vehicle and fumbled frantically with the ignition. The key had been left in, as it had in all the vehicles, to enable their captors to use them with ease.

"Hurry up," Hoeness hissed, not helping the nerves that caused Gabriel to stumble over his actions.

Both men flinched as the windshield of the vehicle starred and shattered. They looked up to see Vladimir—still and silent like a rock while the madness whirled around him—standing before them, about ten yards from the front of the jeep, arm extended with a Beretta 93R in his fist.

The engine of the jeep coughed into life while both scientists sat, seemingly transfixed, by the man before them.

BOLAN MOVED IN on the encampment. Triggering the last of his explosives, he also took short blasts at more moving targets. Another two down, one of them dead and the other uncertain—so far he had been able to even up the numbers a little without getting in too close. That would have to change.

He took a flash grenade from his stock, and used the diversion of the last explosive charge to stand upright and launch it in the direction of the camp. He risked his targets being caught up in the detonation, but it was a chance he would have to take. He was still outnumbered and would need to use any advantage he could take.

He fell to the ground as the grenade arced through the air. There was no fire hitting sand around him, so it was safe to assume that his location had not been spotted in the confusion.

The roar of an explosion and a flash of light that penetrated even through his closed and covered eyes told him that it was time to move. Flashing lights appeared before his eyes as he stood up and started to move toward the camp. He shook his head to clear his vision; he had to be as sharp as possible in order to take out any enemy while locating and securing his targets.

Not a big ask, he thought grimly.

There was no fire on him as he advanced toward the camp. The flash grenade had done its work and the guards were temporarily blinded. It was a relatively easy task for him to pick them off before they had a chance to adjust. But as he got closer to the camp and the numbers of opposition thinned out, it struck him that there was a problem. Among those who were falling easily, he could see no sign of either Russian.

If they were with the two targets, then this could be a much trickier task than he would have liked.

It was then, as the echoes of the grenade blast cleared in his ears, that he realized he could hear two distinct jeep engines whine and roar in the desert air. As the last of the guards fell to his HK G63A4 bursts, he scanned the immediate area and then cursed loudly as he saw the plumed clouds of two jeeps exiting to the west. He couldn't be sure, but it looked like a pursuit rather than a retreat.

There were vehicles left in the compound, which presently resembled a charnel house as he was surrounded by the decimated guard. He headed toward them, knowing that he had no time to waste. With every step the two vehicles escaped him more—the last thing he wanted was to have a firefight on the move, but it looked as if that was the way it was going to be.

GABRIEL HAD BEEN frozen for a moment, seeing the tall Russian framed in the shattered windshield. But then the adrenaline had kicked in and he figured that no matter how valuable he and Hoeness may be, there was every chance that the Russian would just take them out and to hell with his paymasters.

Well, he'd had enough of being ground underfoot. If this was how it was going to end for him, he might as well go out fighting. He hadn't fought so far, and just look where that had gotten him.

He gunned the engine and released the brake, and the jeep shot forward toward the tall Russian. If Gabriel was to stop him from firing at them again, then the only hope was to mow him down.

VLADIMIR STOOD HIS ground for a second, pumping three shots at the shattered windshield and the hood of the vehicle. The shells whined off the metal of the vehicle, and uselessly through the empty windshield as Gabriel ducked down and pushed his fellow scientist flat in his seat.

Swearing loudly, the Russian dove out of the way after pumping the rest of the magazine into the approaching vehicle, blindly hoping to cause damage to man or machine. He was unsuccessful, and rolled across the floor of the camp, bumping into the dead body of one of his men and getting a mouthful of bloodied sand for his trouble.

When he came upright, wiping the sand from his eyes, he could see that the jeep piloted by the scientist had veered wildly, cutting across the tent that should have held the auction, causing it to fall symbolically.

"Vladimir—come on!" Piotr yelled from behind him. Wheeling around, Vladimir could see that the fat man had taken the wheel behind another of the vehicles. He ran across, reloading as he went, and climbed in beside Piotr, who already had the engine running.

"Who the fuck is attacking us?" he yelled.

Vladimir shrugged. "Get going. Whoever they are, they won't follow us."

As their jeep wheeled and spun around in the sand, Vladimir leaned out and took out the tires of the remaining vehicles, two on each, to render them useless. He could hear the chatter of fire and the screams of his men—he had no idea how many were in the assault party, but neither did he care. His men had proved to be of straw when it came to it. The task he and the fat man had left to them was to secure their cargo, and then retreat and regroup in safety.

He reloaded once more as Piotr hit the gas and urged his vehicle on over the desert sands, the engine screaming as he tried to gain ground on the erratic vehicle in front of them that veered wildly as the scientist fought for control.

Behind them, the camp grew silent as the guards were taken out one by one. A pall of smoke and cordite hung over it. Neither of the Russians looked back—it could be written off, as long as they regained their cargo.

But it would have to be paid for, eventually—and not by them.

BOLAN CURSED LOUDLY as he saw the wheels of the vehicles that had been left behind. Two flats on each. There was no way that he would be able to follow the two vehicles that grew smaller on the horizon with each second. He couldn't make up his mind if this was a strategic retreat or if it was some kind of escape attempt by his targets, pursued by the Russians. It would make more sense if it was the former, as that would more readily explain the disabling of the remaining vehicles. And yet there was something about it…

Bolan made a quick survey of the camp. There was no indication of anyone left alive; even those he had only injured had not been able to survive long in the crossfire and with no immediate medical assistance. While this meant that he would encounter no more resistance, it also left him with no one that he could interrogate. Not that they would probably have known much—they were likely just grunts.

Even though he was in no immediate danger, there was still a need for speed. If there was anything left here that would give him intel indicating where they may head next, then the sooner he could get it and return to his own vehicle the better. Part of him cursed his caution in leaving his vehicle so far away, even though this had been in every other way the correct decision.

The tent, only part of which was still erect, revealed nothing except that it had been laid out in a similar manner to the stateroom on the yacht. There were no tents for the men, which suggested that they had not intended to be hanging around too long.

Would it be worth waiting to get a look at the incoming auction bidders? He wondered about this for a moment, then dismissed it. It may be useful for Brognola, but it would get him nowhere in regaining the targets.

The trailer, too, revealed very little. A radio receiver, clothes in a cupboard unit, and the materials taken from the yacht that belonged to the scientists. Whatever happened next, the cartel that was behind this would be forced to conduct the auction without the demonstration materials.

That was a point worth considering—where would they go next? This was assuming that the Russians had taken the scientists with them and not, as seemed possible, that the scientists had used the cover of his attack to try and escape. If they were taken alive, then what?

Too many questions and not enough intel to make a decision. It was a long way back to his own transport, and he was losing ground and time by pondering these questions. Information was what he needed, though it seemed thin on the ground here. He left the trailer and looked around at the silent camp. All that was left were the remaining vehicles. It was a long shot, but there seemed to be little else to hope for. With any luck, the Russians had taken the first vehicle at hand and not necessarily the one they used as a mobile command post—for they must have operated like that, there was no other OP.

It was the second vehicle he searched. The Russians had left a laptop and two smartphones. Unless either of them carried one on his person, then Bolan had lucked into their entire communications and intel system.

He took the three pieces of equipment and secured them on his person. He was still carrying the HK, and intended to keep it handy until he was well clear of the site—which he needed to be soon. Forget that the Russians and the targets were well away—incoming bidders and their security were now a threat. He needed to get back to his own vehicle and his own phone and laptop, which he had purposely left behind.

Squaring himself, Bolan took one last look around before sighting his location and beginning the march back to the deserted farm.

GABRIEL DROVE HARD, but with a sinking feeling. He had no idea in which direction he was headed, and the desert blowing up around him was blinding him as he tried to pilot the vehicle. Beside him, Hoeness was crying. The older man had completely gone to pieces, and in truth Gabriel did not blame him. It was only the fear of what would happen if they stopped and were caught that was making him carry on. Who, looking at them at this moment, would believe that these two disheveled, terrified and cowed men were scientists of international reputation who had researched their way to what they saw as a breakthrough for mankind?

Who gave a shit about mankind right now? Gabriel thought. All he wanted was to live, and not to be frightened. Not necessarily in that order.

He risked looking behind him, the vehicle bucking as he took his eyes off the undulating and treacherous dunes that rose and fell around them. There was no doubt that the other jeep was catching up with them. It drove straighter, truer than Gabriel could pilot his own vehicle. It seemed as though it had a life of its own: implacable. The windshield hid the occupants from view, but at least the Russians had not yet fired on them. That was something—maybe a sign that they would not kill them outright. Perhaps they still had value. Slavery was preferable to death—a bowed and subservient existence better than none at all. Gabriel would never have believed he could have felt that way, but the imminent approach of death had affected him in an unexpected manner.

This panicked train of thought cost their freedom. He turned back to face the front, still distracted, and failed to see a sudden dip in the sands. There was not enough time for him to steer the vehicle out of the drop, and he was thrown forward over the wheel, stalling the vehicle. The air was driven out of him by the impact, and as he tried to draw breath despite aching ribs, he heard the pursuing vehicle slow and come to a halt behind them.

Hoeness was still crying.

PIOTR SAT BEHIND the wheel, his face giving nothing away as he listened to the voice on the other end of his cell phone. Vladimir could not hear the words, but the distant and tinny timbre of the voice coming through to him told him all he needed to know. He sat looking straight ahead, not wanting to embarrass his colleague by catching his eye. Looking ahead through the windshield he could see the rear of the stalled jeep with its tail in the air as it sat in the hollow formed by the dune. There was no sign of movement. He doubted that the crash had been enough to seriously injure the two scientists. Fear was what had paralyzed them—that and a crushing sense of defeat. He doubted they would cause him any further trouble.

They would not have caused him any trouble in the first place if not for whoever had mounted the attack on the encampment; they were the ones who would get payback, when he had the time.

Finally, Piotr snapped his cell shut and sighed.

"What did they say?" Vladimir asked without looking at him.

"As you would expect, we are incompetent dogs who are not worth the money they pay us, and if we fuck up one more time they will have us hunted down like the dogs that we are and have us killed slowly and painfully."

"Yes, of course. They have their tantrums. But what of our orders?"

"Ah, yes. We are dogs who are incompetent but still we must gather the cargo and proceed to an arranged spot where we will be met. From there, a new auction point will be given to us, as it will to those who wish to bid, and we will be assisted to the location. We are still good enough, despite our lowly station, to act as their bodyguards."

"Naturally. They would have to hire us to track ourselves, they know that. I would assume that they also realize that whoever attacked us and facilitated this escape must have obtained our location from a leak?"

"They are angry, not stupid. I think they will be investigating that."

"I also think that they will not rush a second auction," Vladimir said. "They will have to be cautious about security, not just for us, but for those whose cash they hope to extract."

"So you are saying that this may be a good thing in the longer term, yes?" the fat man asked sardonically.

"Of course. Everything can be worked to your advantage if you think about it," Vladimir replied with a humor that his face did not betray. "Now, if you will excuse me, I have some work to do."

He got out of the jeep, drawing the Beretta 93R and keeping it in both hands, pointed down, as he advanced on the dunes. Proscribing an arc, he half slid, half walked down the shifting sand, keeping his balance with an ease that betrayed his training. When he drew level with the side door of the jeep, he lifted the Beretta up so that it was level with the door.

"Come out," he said in German. "Slowly. No stupidity. No time wasting. You have nowhere to go, eh?"

He waited. There was no sign of movement from within, but he remained—gun leveled, posture steady. Eventually, the door opened and Gabriel crawled out. He looked beaten. He stood in front of Vladimir, head bowed. After a short wait, Hoeness followed, coming out on his hands and knees. He had stopped crying—there was nothing left—but he was shaking.

Vladimir looked at them. They were pathetic. But they were his job.

"On your feet," he barked at Hoeness. When the scientist did not respond, the Russian snapped at Gabriel. "Help him."

The younger scientist helped the older one into a semi-crouching position, and they shuffled toward the jeep where Piotr was waiting.

"I'll be glad when this is fucking over." Vladimir sighed as he watched them go.

BOLAN HAD REACHED his jeep in double time, and was taking a brief and cursory look at the phones and the laptop while he called Stony Man Farm from his own phone. He cut off Kurtzman's greeting and briefly outlined what had happened.

"Uploading now," Bolan said as he relayed the information on the laptop hard disk to Stony Man Farm. "Listen, these guys will be desperate to get this completed, but I've had a long march back to think about it, and they're not going to be hurrying unnecessarily. They're also going to realize Hal has a mole in their camp, so things may get tight. The way they've proceeded before, the logical move would be Israel. But I can't see them wanting to cross swords with the Israelis. Egypt is possible, but I'd put cash money on Libya. There's still enough chaos in the transitional council for them to find holes."

"I'll get on to what you've sent. Anything we can take from it that can be traced back to the Russians, or get us hacked into their networks, I'll let you know."

"Make it soon, Bear. I'm heading back to the border. I'll need men next time, and I know who I can rely on."

"You can take them with you?"

"If there's a way, then Jared will know it. It's just a matter of logistics."

"I'll tell Hal that if a bill comes in," Kurtzman said before signing off.

Bolan sat for a brief moment, looking at the cell phone, before sighing and putting the jeep into gear.

"I'll be glad to see the back of this one," he said to himself, little realizing how he echoed his adversary.

11

"Cooper, I have to admit I didn't think I'd be seeing you alive again. But then again, I didn't think that if I did see you it would be alone, either," Jared Hassim shrugged as Bolan arrived at the rendezvous. The other two Arab fighters looked on impassively.

"Things did not go exactly according to plan," Bolan said wryly. "Not that they ever do, I guess. But it does mean that I may have some use for you."

"If the price is right," Hassim replied in a deceptively offhand manner. "I would rather we discuss this elsewhere. It feels a little uncomfortable to be so close to the border carrying so much hardware. Anyone who happens along may not be as understanding as I would like."

Bolan was agreeable. It made sense for them to move, and it would also save him time—even though they may spend hours traveling, minutes could still matter.

"Drive with me," he said. "I'll brief you on the way."

Hassim joined Bolan, and the two vehicles turned and headed on the long journey back to the fishing village. It was a long drive to the coast, and Bolan was bone weary after the combination of combat and travel. Despite this, he took first shift at the wheel, carefully briefing his companion on the events that had taken place. Hassim's eyebrows shot up when he realized that the targets had probably been the architects of their own failure to be freed, but refrained from comment until Bolan had completed his monologue.

"Matt," he said slowly, with Bolan noting the change of address and its implications. "Those halfwits chose a stupid time to grow a pair. That's the kind of lousy luck that loses wars," he continued, his early American years seeping back into his speech. "Russians, they get all the luck."

Bolan grimaced. "Those guys on the ground? They're soldiers, just like us. They just work for whoever pays top dollar. I don't care where they come from—I just need to take them down. I'll need your men, if they're willing. And if I'm right, it'll be a long haul."

"Ah, we've got nothing better to do," Hassim joked. "Besides, the cash is always useful. If I was them I would be shitting myself and want to get the sale done before the buyers get bored with the haggling and wander away. It should be a simple enough mission."

Bolan held his peace. He didn't agree, but this was not the time to argue. They pulled up, switched drivers, and Bolan settled into the back of the jeep to grab some sleep. Yet his mind still raced, with half an ear out for his phone—as soon as Kurtzman could update him, he'd feel a lot better.

VLADIMIR FELT MUCH the same. Jordan was not a hot zone. Any unrest grumbled below the surface, and the royal family was determined to keep their people at peace with a degree of Western liberalism. Despite this, there was still a military presence in some of the areas that bordered the West Bank, and heading into densely populated Irbid put them right in the middle of that region. If their cargo had been decently dressed and behaving normally, both Russians would have been confident. But they were still in ragged clothing and were *not* behaving normally. The older man was withdrawn and muttering softly to himself. The younger one was downcast and broken. They would attract attention if their vehicle was stopped. And any search would, of course, reveal ordnance that required explanation.

"If they want us to do a good job, why do they force us to take such risks?" Vladimir asked coldly. "It would make much more sense to send someone out to us with provision and transport so we could take a wider path and avoid this type of area."

Piotr sighed as he guided the vehicle through the outskirts of a city whose buildings and roads contrasted dramatically with the desolation they had so recently left behind.

"They do not care for such things. They are not soldiers. They are panicking. We must make the most of what we are given to work with."

Piotr's resigned tone spoke more than his words. It would only add to their load if Vladimir continued to complain, so Piotr remained in silence while he used the GPS to guide them to a backstreet garage where two Arabs were looking out for them. Guiding them in and securing the doors, the Arabs waited until Piotr killed the engine before hitting the lights.

From the outside it had appeared as nothing more than a cheap backstreet chop-shop, with a battered sign and a peeling paint facade. With the interior hidden from the street, the strip lighting across the length of the ceiling revealed a workshop that was immaculately maintained. There were two other vehicles in the garage—an ancient Mercedes truck with a canvas back that was battered and pitted but had an open hood revealing a customised engine; and a Humvee with a mounted M249 SAW 5.56 mm.

"I can see why you like privacy," Vladimir said by way of greeting, indicating the two vehicles.

"It pays to be careful," one of the Arabs replied. Both were young men, bearded and with faces that were carefully trained to betray little. It was only by their body language that Vladimir determined the man in command.

"We have been given this location, but no further orders. Do you have any?" he asked.

The Arab shook his head. "We are to provide you with cover until we receive word. Then we use the truck to convey you to the next location. That has, I think, not been determined."

"Good. We could both use a shower and food. The merchandise needs to be cleaned up a little, too," Vladimir said, indicating the two scientists in the rear of the jeep.

The Arab peered in, then back at him. "They are what all the fuss is about?"

Vladimir shrugged. "I agree. But that is not our concern. We just need to get them to the next location in one piece and, frankly, looking good even if they are shit, you know?"

The Arab shook his head, coughing a short laugh. "Okay. We will do our best."

"I'VE BEEN DOING my best with it—we all have—but they're fast, Striker. In many ways."

Bolan rubbed his forehead. He was sitting in the building he had left just over twenty-four hours before on his way to Jordan, and he felt as though he was reliving the previous day.

"I would have expected that. They must have known they'd left the phones and laptop behind. The first thing I'd expect them to do is put up new firewalls."

"Naturally—and they're very good. There's no back door that anyone here has found, but we did manage to extract a contact list from the email account before it went down. It makes for very interesting reading. The usual suspects, of course, but it was a little saddening to see some names from our own neck of the woods on there." There was a satirical edge to his voice. "However, sad to say even more that we could not get at what those names have been returning. Hal has them, but what he can do is limited, especially in the short time available."

"Listen, Bear, if we know who organized this hijack of the sale, then that's fine and Hal can deal with that later. That's not my concern. I need to know where the hell I'm headed next, and how long I have to get there."

There was a pause on the other end of the line. "That's kind of what I meant by their being fast in a lot of ways. Hal's mole is dead. His car had a sudden brake failure."

"Won't that look a little suspicious?"

"Yeah, well, it was more like they failed to stop him when a ten tonner hit a red light and took him out with a sideswipe. Drunk driver."

"You can buy a lot of liquor and an easy jail life with what he must have gotten."

"Exactly. Thing is, with the mole gone, Hal can't move on the names we've got in Washington until we've hacked their email."

Bolan knew what this meant. Enforced downtime until the rendezvous was made and the appropriate email hacked. "Okay. Just keep informed."

He disconnected and relayed the information to Hassim and his men. There was a tension in the air that was difficult to dispel. When they reached the village and Hassim put the proposition to the men, there had been little hesitation in their agreement. Bolan could pay well from his war chest, and in truth some of the men felt cheated of the action they had been expecting on their earlier excursion. Combat and the adrenaline rush could be a drug. But now they were sitting around, waiting—and that was the worst feeling. Some gambled, others prayed. One or two disappeared outside the main building. Hassim told them to rest up, be ready—not so easy when they were hyped up and ready to roll.

Bolan was sure the Russians would be headed to Libya, but Hassim couldn't see it. He said, "Matt, I am a simple man and I believe in a simple man's ways. If you have produce to sell, you do not tell your buyer to follow you across half the fucking continent. Egypt has plenty of places to hide two men and some soldiers." There was little point in Bolan trying to get the mercenary leader to listen to a battle plan until the destination was settled. So all he could do was sit and wait, and mull it over in his own mind.

If it was Libya, then which part of the country would be most likely? Great swaths of it were desert, like Jordan. There were also areas of oasis, raised on plateaus, and because these were isolated from each other they tended not to gather towns and cities. Oil was more important than water. The oil regions were those with the densest populations. If he was back in a Washington bar he would bet any money on the north of the country, where there were some oases and not a lot else. That also took them to a coastal region, and with a no-fly zone anywhere near water it made things a whole lot easier to set up. How long would it take the team to get there by boat? Come to that, how long would it take to procure a seaworthy vessel for such a journey?

There was a lot to think about and the clearer he had it in his mind, the quicker he could relay it to Hassim when the moment came. Except that fate—and Kurtzman—had other ideas. His train of thought was interrupted by the ring of his cell.

"Bear—speak to me."

"You got it right. Libya. Twenty-eight hours. Nearest coastal city where you could land is Derna, and the rendezvous is a good eight hours over the desert, down to the southwest. Man, it's mostly desert—"

"Most of it is over there," Bolan interjected.

"Damn right, Striker. Point is that you don't have a lot of time to get over there, especially as flying is a no-no. I've sent you the details and maps that you'll need. We don't have much on the ground there—it's still chaos with the NTC, and—"

"That's okay, I have what I need." He paused. "There is one thing, Bear. If Hal's mole is down, then—"

"Striker, you wouldn't believe who came up on that damn list. Hal has the details, though what he can do with it other than cover his own ass I don't know. What I do know is that you should watch your back."

"Friendly fire?"

"I don't know about that. I do know that it's likely the Russians could back-engineer and figure out who hacked them. Whether they can do it before the auction takes place is another matter."

Bolan nodded to himself. "Fine. Guess we know where we are. I'll set up my boys, and maintain silence unless I need something real fast. You couldn't manage a UN air strike at short notice if I need one, I suppose?"

"Hey, we can hack anything and send the order. Doesn't mean it can't be traced."

"Yeah, but that would be when it was too late." Bolan smiled. "I wouldn't do that to you, Bear."

"Unless it was really necessary," Kurtzman replied with heavy emphasis. "The impossible just takes a little longer, Striker. You take it easy out there."

Bolan signed off, took a deep breath and looked back to the village.

Time to roll.

"Colonel, it's good to see you again…"

Colonel Tom Osterman shook the proffered hand and

looked around. It was late evening, and the Mall was almost deserted. In the shadow of the Supreme Commander, he felt uneasy at this meeting, no matter how high the clearance of the man before him.

"Make this quick, Senator. There are too many eyes and ears," Osterman whispered, not realizing this was hardly an original observation.

"Most of them are ours, Colonel. This concerns Chronos."

Osterman's gut churned. Black ops and hidden budgets had been the bane of his life since becoming a desk jockey. Trouble was, you could hide paperwork and figures but you couldn't unlearn…too many people knew exactly how deeply he was involved, even though all he yearned for was retirement and a pension.

"I—I wasn't aware of your involvement—"

"No, possibly not. But I was certainly aware of yours. You only have six months until you retire. It would be a shame if that was dogged by rumor and an official investigation that may possibly even cause you—"

"I get it, Senator. What do you need?"

"As you are aware, Chronos is heavily reliant on nuclear technology. This is expensive and cumbersome. Currently we are trying to obtain the sole rights to a process that may solve our current problems. There are other interested parties, but we are confident that we can outbid them."

"Then I don't see—"

The senator sighed. "It's quite simple. Another private project within our governmental structure has an interest in stopping the auction for this property going ahead. We need someone to ensure that the sale is not interrupted. It is important for our own needs that this seem to be a legitimate—if you will excuse the term under such conditions—auction. You see what I mean?"

There was a pause. Osterman knew too well, and was

unwilling to voice either his understanding or his objection. The senator realized this.

"Let me put it more simply, Colonel. You will send a covert task force to prevent our representatives from disrupting the sale."

"Go up against our own." It was a statement of disgust rather than a question.

"It may be distasteful to you, but it is necessary for your own well-being as much as the project's. Let me put it this way. Are you familiar with Camus?" The senator smiled at the colonel's puzzled expression. "No, perhaps not. I mention him because I once saw a play where a man returned to an isolated inn after many years away. He was thought dead, I believe, and his mother and sister had spent the intervening years robbing and killing their guests. He wished to surprise them and so did not at first reveal his identity. Unfortunately, it was only after his death, on examining his billfold, that they discovered the truth. It was called *Cross Purposes,* which is as apt a description as I can think of. You understand me, of course?"

Osterman thought of his log cabin by the lake and his grandchildren sharing their summer vacations with him.

"It will be done," he said finally, with only the slightest crack in his voice betraying his true feelings.

THE IPAD SAT center of the table while Bolan indicated the location of the auction and detailed his plan. They would set up camp on the edge of the Qattara Depression, which would place them about thirty klicks from their enemy's location. When he pointed out Derna as a likely landing point, he was interrupted by Hassim.

"Just along the coast, up near Egypt, is Tobruk. Less busy. Fewer prying eyes. You follow?"

Bolan assented. "Good idea. Apt, too." He smiled when

he caught Hassim's puzzled expression. "Military history, World War Two. Rommel and the Nazi panzer divisions ruled the desert, and by rights should never have been defeated. They reckoned without the British general, Montgomery. His forces were smaller, their hardware not so adaptable. But he had balls, and he knew overweening arrogance when he saw it. He out-thought Rommel, and that's what we're going to have to do. They might have more men than last time—hell, they'd be damned stupid not to—but their attention will be split between the possibility of our assault, and maintaining order in a bunch of bidders who may just be spitting blood by now. We have to take advantage of that. Superior force can always be overturned by surprise and intelligence."

Hassim looked at his men. "Matt Cooper, you just better hope you have brains, 'cause I can't vouch for me and my boys," he said with a sly grin.

VLADIMIR AND PIOTR were much happier men. Cleaned up, and with their charges also cleaned up and fed, they had been taken in the camo truck to the rendezvous with the vessel that would take them from their port side destination out into the Mediterranean and toward Libya. From the outside it seemed to be a down-at-heel cargo boat of medium size, flying a Liberian flag. It could have been any one of a dozen idling at dockside while their crews killed time until they could find a non-Muslim port and drink their wages away. And while it was true that it was, in a sense, a cargo boat that would relay a most valuable load across the water, that was where the resemblance ended once the two Russians and their charges were aboard.

Although the bridge appeared to be weather-beaten and rusting from the outside, the interior contained state-of-the-art equipment and communications equipment that was military in origin. Similarly, when the Russians went aboard they were interested, rather than surprised, to see that the tawdry exterior belied a below deck set-up that housed cabins for both crew and a number of passengers, with much of the cargo space taken up by extra cabin space and a fully equipped armory. Much of the above deck container space was taken up by dummies that could be stripped back to reveal mounted gun and cannon emplacements similar to that of military vessels of comparable size.

Below decks, after they had been shown their bunks for the journey and their charges were secured, the Russians were taken to the captain. He relayed their destination, plans for their travel into the interior of the Libyan desert to the Qattarra region and the main oasis where, even as they spoke, forces had been advanced to set up and secure the site where the merchandise would be auctioned. On board the ship were six men who were detailed to accompany them on the road trip across the desert to the location. Another half-dozen men were on board as security in the event of any attempted intervention.

This time, it seemed to the two Russians, their paymasters had taken into account possible danger and disruption and left little to chance.

"I prefer it that way," Piotr said as the two men stood on the forward deck, looking across the Mediterranean as the prow split the deceptively calm waters. He hawked and spat into the wash below them.

"I would prefer it to be finished," Vladimir said flatly. "We are better prepared, but I have a bad feeling in my gut."

"I, too, have never liked Arab food," Piotr said straight-faced. It was only when the taller man gave him a cold stare that his face cracked. "Vladimir, I have never understood your unrelenting pessimism. Of course there is always risk. But if you are ready, and have the greater firepower, then you have all the advantage you need."

"I just hope you are right," the scarred soldier muttered.

BOLAN WENT ON trust and past example in relying on the resourcefulness of the men he was working with—and they did not prove him wrong. After loading ordnance into the jeeps, they drove a short distance from the fishing village to an inlet where, under the shelter of a rock outcrop and docked at the bottom of a winding path, stood a fishing smack that was like any of those in the village they had left.

"There have been some prying eyes, Matt. For this reason, it was a precaution to move this boat. You will see why." Hassim had told him with a wink when they hiked down the path, each of the fourteen men shouldering a burden.

"I'm more concerned with our transport when we get to Tobruk," Bolan returned.

"I have friends there. That is why I would rather there than Derna. In Tobruk I know I can lay hands on what we need. For a price, of course."

"Of course," Bolan said wryly.

They were now on the small wooden dock and watched the loading. Hassim beckoned Bolan to follow him onto the vessel, and after they had stowed their load, they went back up onto the bridge.

"I don't get it," Bolan said in an amused tone. "Why hide this one? It doesn't look like it's any different from any other smack."

Hassim grinned broadly. "Of course not. That would be incredibly stupid. But then again, if a suspicious man took a closer look, as they sometimes do, he would see why a little subterfuge was necessary."

Bolan looked more closely at the controls of the vessel. "Show me the engines," he asked, realization dawning. Led below deck, he could see that the small, functional engine of the smack as originally constructed had been removed. In its place were turbo engines that could propel such a small vessel at a rate that would eat up the waterways.

"Naturally, we had to reinforce the hull. This, too, would be obvious with more than a casual examination. Otherwise, it is as it was built. No armaments, no fancy computerized shit. You can take that on and off at will. This has one function only—speed."

The two men returned to the deck. Hassim's men had loaded, cast off and were settling in for the journey. The smack wasn't built for great comfort, but as it moved out of the small inlet and into the main body of the water, gathering speed as it hit greater depth, Bolan realized that with any luck they would have little time to relax—only time to prepare for the fight to come.

His cell phone buzzing interrupted this train of thought.

"Striker—something very strange is happening. There's a UN flight on its way. There's so much fog around any intel, that I get a very bad feeling about this."

"Bear, if you can't get to the root of what's going on, then the only sensible thing to assume is that it's trouble. Where's it headed?"

"Three guesses."

OSTERMAN HAD RELUCTANTLY called in all the favors he had left. If the senator wanted anything else before the colonel's retirement came around, then he truly would have to whistle. Sitting in his office at the Pentagon, Osterman reviewed his career and reluctantly came to the conclusion that it was about to come crashing down ignominiously around his ears, one way or another. Whichever way he turned, he was out of options. As he sighed, stood up, and left his office, he knew that he had set in motion a chain of events that were now beyond his recall.

Leaving Egypt and heading for Tripoli was a UN plane carrying troops who were being briefed on a mission they believed was about maintaining security in the region. That would soon be an obvious sham to them, but they would still fight as long as they had their orders.

Osterman had a pretty shrewd idea who was behind the other U.S. activity in the region. He knew who he would rather have at his back. Added to which, they were both homing in on an auction that broke so many international laws that it would take a team of lawyers a good decade to even get started.

It was not going to be pretty. Osterman yearned for his log cabin by the lake. Somehow, he'd be surprised if he ever got there again.

FOR VLADIMIR AND Piotr, it was a pleasingly efficient journey to the oasis site that had been chosen for the auction. Coming ashore at Derna had been simple, the requisite number of U.S. dollars having changed hands. Their charges were resigned to their fate, and neither said anything at all—not even in communication with each other—during the journey. Desert-worthy vehicles were ready for the Russians and their accompanying guard. Within half an hour of landing they were at the edge of the desert and on their way.

FOR BOLAN AND his mercenary crew, the journey was also simple, if lacking in the more material comforts. Docking at Tobruk, Hassim greeted the harbormaster as an old friend— which, as the man was married to his wife's sister, was not surprising. Then they quickly loaded up the jeeps that had been supplied for them by the harbormaster, who had been careful to make tracing any movements as difficult as possible.

Bolan handed over the cash required, and they set off across the desert toward their own destination, located just outside the oasis region chosen for the auction. Here they would set up camp and prepare for their attack. Hours passed for them in journey and inaction, as they did for the Russians. Tension simmered beneath the surface as the endless dry lands gave them little to ponder other than the forthcoming firefight.

LANDING AT TRIPOLI, the UN plane disgorged a detachment of U.S. Marines under orders to root out and eliminate two rebel groups that would clash over intel that would tilt the balance of power in the region. Their briefing told them that they were to secure two men—clearly marked and indentified—who held the intel, and to terminate with prejudice any forces that got between them and their target. They were also told that there may be rogue American forces at work, and to disregard nationality. Anyone who was not in their detachment was to be treated as hostile. They were good soldiers who had no idea that they were on a black ops mission. They were determined to fulfill their brief as they loaded up and shipped out for the road journey to their objective.

PIOTR AND VLADIMIR arrived at their destination, gratified to see that their paymasters had learned from their recent errors, and that the site of the auction was fenced by motion detectors and cameras as well as patrolled by a force that—with the addition of the men who had traveled with them—was twice the strength of the one in Jordan. After an inspection and debriefing with the ex-Gaddafi general who had been hired to head up security, they settled their charges in a trailer that was guarded by two assigned gunmen. It was only then that the ex-military man indicated they should follow him to the tent that served as mission base.

"Gentlemen, I have received this communication. I think you should read it," he said in clipped, heavily accented English before turning a laptop screen to them. Vladimir allowed Piotr to read the communication.

"Well?" he said when the fat man had signaled his completion of the email with a snort.

"It seems that you may have a chance to extract payment for what happened in Jordan."

"They know where we are?"

"Whoever employs them, much as we are ourselves employment, has hacked our paymasters' communications. They know our location. Of course, by the same token, our paymasters have been able to back-engineer that hacking, find their own backdoor and inform us of where they can be found."

"They will, of course, be aware of this?"

Piotr shrugged. "Perhaps not. Not yet. But still we should assume as much. It may be as well to preempt them and neutralize a threat while extracting some revenge."

Vladimir smiled coldly. "This is something that I could like very much."

12

Present day

The crackling radio signal came through. "We lose contact with two. Others circle and close. Orders?"

Vladimir drew back his lips in a mirthless grin that was more of a snarl. "I want some alive. I have matters to settle."

Piotr raised an eyebrow. "We send in a force half their size, lose a third, and you want prisoners?"

"Toying with them," the tall Russian shrugged. "Having fun."

"This is not the time to do that," Pitor snapped at him. "They should be eliminated. We are not here to run risks."

"What risks? They have lost men, they will lose more. We already outnumber them here. We have excellent security precautions in place. And we have a man—" here he indicated the general "—who knows a little about the extraction of information. Why not? After the problems they have caused, a little relaxation may be pleasant."

Piotr sighed. "Very well." He leaned forward to deliver his orders. The men had been sent out with ancient tech so that any capture or decease would leave a false marker of technical capability. As far as Piotr was concerned, this was another unnecessary conceit on the part of his compatriot—but he knew very well how difficult Vladimir could be if crossed, and his cooperation was a continuing requirement. As he spoke clearly and concisely to the straining ears of the men in the field, Piotr hoped that technical and language issues would not cause a last-minute stumble.

If so, then he would finally have to call time on Vladimir. And he did not wish to do such a thing after so many years.

BOLAN AND HASSIM marshaled their men in the center of the camp. The grenades had caused chaos and made it hard for them to direct forces, as it had made any kind of accurate estimate of the enemy hard to ascertain. Bolan worked on the assumption that there had been four pairs of men at regular compass points and that two pairs had been eliminated. Three directions of attack, then, and probably six men—the attackers were outnumbered, but against this they had the darkness and the front foot as impetus.

He barked at Hassim's men, directing three pairs of them to strike out in the direction of remaining fire while the rest set up covering fire. They were pinned down and ripe to be picked off unless they took the offensive.

Sami and Husni would circle north, Rafik and Aref would take the south, and Riad and Kamal would cover the remaining compass points. Their orders were simple—exterminate with extreme prejudice. It was vital that they wipe out this opposition. As they sited the directions from which fire was emanating and started their crawl toward the enemy, Bolan and Hassim directed the remaining men to lay down a concentrated stream of suppressing fire that would hold the enemy to the positions located by their own fire. As this proceeded, Bolan used the RPG-7 that they had brought with them to send out a series of shrapnel grenades that would possibly do some damage, but would certainly help in pinning the enemy down to one position. He was cautious with the grenades as their ordnance was limited, and picked his spots with care.

The tactic was obviously working. As the seconds ticked by, the fire raining back on them in return grew sparse, dwindling to a trickle as the focus of the action shifted to the darkness of the dunes. The men in the camp were reduced to the status of onlookers as flashes of fire and the distant chatter of SMG fire described a firefight in which they could be nothing more than onlookers due to the risk of taking out their own men.

Even this distant fire—observed from three compass points as an obscene light show—dwindled into silence, and the men in the camp fell into a tense silence as they waited.

Sami and Husni returned over the sands, triumphant. Sami carried weapons and communications equipment that he dumped in the center of camp. Hassim picked up the ancient tech and gave Bolan a puzzled look.

"This?" he queried. "Old shit, Cooper. Not like our boys at all."

Bolan said nothing, pondering the situation. His ruminations were interrupted by the return of Riad and Kamal, who also carried the old comm equipment and some ordnance with them.

Bolan picked up one of the old radios. It crackled impotently. "Either we just got unlucky and were attacked by a bunch of desperados on the make, or our target force is trying to throw us off the scent. This isn't the kind of thing I would expect from them. Maybe that's the point." He looked up with a sudden realization. "Where are Rafik and Aref?"

Hassim looked concerned. "If these kids are back, they should be. Unless…"

Bolan organized the search party. It was still night-black in the desert, silent and forbidding as he and two others swept out in an arc to cover the area of the last firefight. He expected to find the corpses of the two older fighters, perhaps with one of their enemy. Certainly one must have gotten away if both of Hassim's men had been taken out. And yet, despite the signs of combat, and a dark splattering revealed by flash to be the blood of at least one man, there was no sign of anyone living or dead.

The party of three men congregated then returned to the camp empty-handed to be met by a grim-faced Jared. He held up one of the old walkie-talkies.

"This shit is still working. They're not answering, but they know I can hear because I've tried to send. That's why they're doing it."

"Doing what?" Bolan asked, though he was certain he knew the answer.

"They've got my boys. We need to move now, as they know where we are, but I'll tell you this—they'll know our plans. One way or another," he added meaningfully. "But we're going to get them first, Cooper." He fixed Bolan with a stare that determined no argument.

"No one fucks with my boys. We die fighting, fine. That's the risk we take. But not this shit. This is personal, now."

"WILL HE LIVE long enough to verify whatever his piece-of-shit friend says?" Piotr asked Vladimir as they stood in front of Aref. The old fighter was trussed to a chair, his wounds staunched and roughly patched. He had lost a lot of blood on the thirty-kilometer journey to the auction site, and was barely conscious. Unaware, even, of the electrodes attached to his testicles and wired up to a battery that the Libyan ex-general had on a small table, attached to a voltage meter.

Vladimir shrugged. "I don't really care. They will follow, we know where they are located and their likely routes, and so we will be able to face off with them. If we get any detail from these two assholes, then so much the better. Truthfully, it will just make me feel better to see this scum suffer before they die. Carry on with the interrogation."

Piotr's face remained set. He had no objection to torture, per se, but felt that this was wasting time and effort, and was—perhaps more worryingly—another example of Vladimir letting his feelings overrule his professionalism.

Piotr slapped Aref hard across the face to bring him out of his semiconscious delirium. He barked a question at him, which the wounded man seemed to have trouble understanding beneath the fog of pain. Piotr gestured, and the Libyan smiled slyly as he twisted the voltage meter, watching his Arab victim writhe and wail in sudden agony, trying to lift himself from the chair and away from the source of pain, but unable to do so because of his bonds and his own diminishing strength. Piotr slapped him again, barked another question that was answered only by a scream of pain as the Libyan gleefully increased the voltage.

It was going nowhere, and it took only a few minutes for the combination of his injuries and the shock treatment to take its toll on Aref's constitution, his heart unable to take the strain.

Piotr sighed heavily as he gestured for his men to untie the corpse and dispose of it, replacing him with the terrified Rafik. The wizened and battle-hardened man was no coward in combat, and had been taken relatively unharmed only after a blow to the head during hand-to-hand had blacked him out. However, this was not combat—he was powerless at the hands of men who would cause him slow pain with no chance to fight back. He had heard his friend and fellow fighter die. He had no intention of giving them anything, but this did not quell the fear that rose in his breast as he was pushed into the chair, secured and connected to the battery.

Vladimir stepped forward, grinning mirthlessly. He could see the fear in the old man's face, even though Rafik fought to keep his face still as stone. Vladimir came up close, looked Rafik in the eye and laughed gently.

"Tell me and it'll be quick," he taunted. He was rewarded with a glob of phlegm in the face as the old man made what he knew would be his last show of defiance.

Vladimir betrayed no emotion as he stepped back, straightening and wiping the spit away with a tissue. He said nothing to betray the anger inside as he nodded to the Libyan, and the first charge wracked the old man's genitals.

"I haven't even asked him a question as yet," Piotr said mildly.

"Ask him now," Vladimir snapped, indicating the Libyan should kill the charge. "I doubt he'll talk. Scared but stubborn. Perhaps if he were not the enemy, I may admire his stance. Perhaps…"

He stepped back and indicated that Piotr take over questioning. The fat Russian asked a few questions regarding the strength of the opposition force, their armaments and their battle plan. Each was met with a stoic silence broken only by agonized screams of pain as the charge was sent through Rafik's lower body once more, each time increasing in strength. After the last, he blacked out, and with some irritation Vadimir slapped the Arab until he came around. He was rewarded with a barely audible comment on his mother's facility with donkeys.

Vladimir stepped back, wordlessly striding to where the Libyan sat. He brushed him aside and turned the voltage up, allowing the charge to continue as the Arab writhed and squirmed, his screams becoming frail as pain sapped the strength from his body. The air was filled with the stench of burning hair and flesh mixed with the voiding of the Arab's bowels as Rafik passed into merciful unconsciousness.

Piotr reached across and killed the current, taking his compatriot's hand from the battery.

"Enough. We have work to do, without this distraction. Our men will be ready for any attack. We know they have been reduced by two men at least. If there are more casualties or wounded they have to carry, then so much the better. Now we must prepare, yes?"

Vladimir took a last look at the now barely breathing Arab and assented. He allowed Piotr to lead him away, not noticing the signal that passed between the Libyan and the fat Russian. It was only when they were outside the tent that he heard the single shot.

A SINGLE TRUCK moved across the desert sands, its oddly lurching motion revealing the shifting of the sands beneath its heavy wheels. Inside was a detachment of Marines briefed for action. They knew of two objectives. The first was to neutralize the two forces they would be ranged against. The second was to take two men from the danger zone and transport them back to U.S. soil. They were twenty-five miles from their objective.

THE MORNING SUN lit the camp and enabled Bolan and Hassim to take stock of their men and hardware. The battle of the night before had been short and sharp. There were two missing, two dead, and although Shadeeb was in better condition that he had feared, he was still not up to speed. Nine fit men and one operating at a disadvantage. It was not what Bolan would have preferred. But on the upside, they hadn't used as much of their ordnance as he had feared during the firefight, and they were still well equipped.

They pitched camp and loaded up, heading for the auction site, thirty klicks across the desert. It would be hard to hide when they got close, and an all-out frontal assault was their best option. All the more so as their enemy knew their starting location. Rafik and Aref were good men, almost certainly gone, and even if they had talked—which was unlikely—they knew nothing that the enemy couldn't have already guessed.

As the two jeeps rattled across the desert sands toward their fate, Bolan took stock of his men. Hassim's mien set the tone—the Arab mercenaries had a personal involvement in this now that went beyond cash. There would be no doubts about their ferocity—it would just be a matter of whether or not they would let rage color their actions.

It would help if he could gain some intel on the layout of the enemy camp. Bolan took out his smartphone. He had been unwilling to use it as it could be tracked, but it was too late to worry about that. After the preliminaries, he asked if Stony Man Farm had picked up any extra intel that could be of use.

"Striker, they shut up on us tighter than a gnat's ass. Moreover, they hacked us so easily I'm starting to wonder just who is behind these Russians, or who they're working with. Oligarchs can buy a shitload of tech, but there are some things that the military just doesn't let out easily. And they look like they've got that. Hal's onto their Washington connection, hopefully before they get his ass. You need to watch your back. That UN flightload is headed your way, too."

"To stop us?"

"I don't know. Stop you, disrupt the auction—"

"Both," Bolan interjected. "It's best to assume that, I guess. Everyone is an enemy unless actions prove otherwise."

"I'm sorry I can't be of more help. All I can tell you is they're good—very good."

Bolan ended the call. It was no more than he had expected, in truth; their enemy had been one jump ahead all the way along, and the only reason they were able to play catch-up was because the opposition had stopped moving.

He looked at the mileage on the jeep's odometer. Only five miles to go. Showtime.

SUNRISE ALSO BROUGHT a sense of foreboding for the two scientists as the rays penetrated the shades of their trailer window. Since being brought here, the two men had tried to sleep, but neither had been able to get anything more than a fitful rest. Piotr had visited them the previous night and had briefed them on what was expected of them. They were to deliver the same presentation that they had prepared for the original auction. When Hoeness pointed out that they did not have the laptop that contained all their data and slideshow material, the fat Russian had laughed in his face and hit him.

"We are not selling a laptop, fool. That is just window-dressing. Our clients will only want to know that you are alive, sane and available to take up where you left off. We are not selling the idea—they are already sold on that, or else they would not be here. We are selling you. Get that into your heads and at least you will walk out of here to some kind of life. If you fail, and our clients do not make bids, then we will be left with you. A lot of time and money has gone into procuring you and bringing you here. Those who employ myself and Vladimir will not be pleased…either with you, or with us. They will want you disposed of, and believe me, my friend, if they also want a piece of our ass then we will make sure that you suffer for us…"

Neither scientist had said anything, but they had heard the screams of two other men echo in the night, and then the finality of the pistol shot. That had been a partial cause of their fitful rest. They had no doubt that the fat Russian would be as good as his word. The only thing that concerned them both—though neither would say it to the other—was whether or not the traumas of the last few days had caused them to be so shocked that they would lose any rationality. Feeling like they were living in a nightmare, both men felt as though they had lost touch with themselves.

They showered and dressed without exchanging a word. It was only when they heard the desert air split by the sound of choppers in the distance that Gabriel turned to Hoeness.

"I don't think I can do this. I barely know who I am anymore. And I think I might rather that the nightmare ended than carry on, no matter what that means."

The older man shook his head. "You say that, but facing death makes me want to cling more to life, no matter how insane it might seem. If you cannot talk, then for the sake of God do not hinder me. I am so scared I could talk for both of us."

THE PIECE OF equipment Bolan pulled from his duffel bag was small and delicate—in truth it was a surprise that it had come this far unscathed—and Hassim looked at it with interest.

"Matt, I've not seen one of those before."

Bolan's teeth bared in what would, under any other circumstances, been a grin. "Hear that? Look," he said, gesturing in the direction they were headed. "Incoming. We haven't got time to be delicate about this. I'm betting they've got motion sensors and cameras buried around here, just waiting to tip them off. Ordinarily, we'd stop and dig them out. No time for that now, but at least we can see where they are, know how much notice they've got of us coming."

The detector would not tell him much when used in this way, serving only the purpose he had stated. The one good thing about having to approach in this way, with the attendees for the auction approaching, was that the forces of their opponents would be divided between their customers and their oncoming attackers.

For there was little doubt that they would be running straight into the middle of the auction they had come to prevent. Three choppers were approaching the enemy camp. All three were UH-1D Hueys. Crewed by two men, they each held fourteen passengers. That made for forty-two passengers, representatives of up to twenty nation states, with one bodyguard apiece. He seriously doubted that they would have been allowed more than that. Somewhere in there was a U.S. black-ops bidder, representing a part of the government of which even the legislature was probably ignorant.

The Hueys were identical and carried no identifying marks. Bolan figured that they had beat the no-fly zone by the simple expedient of coming from the coast and keeping low after picking up their passengers from a prearranged point. There would be little opportunity for the NTC's new Libyan Republic air force to even realize they were airborne, let alone intercept them, in the short time they were up. That was always assuming that blind eyes had not been paid for, anyway.

"Got it," he yelled as the choppers passed over a seemingly empty stretch of sand. "Impulses from remotes, looks like they're strung around, but they begin and end as early warning here... They now know we're inside," he affirmed to Hassim.

"Fine. Let's rack up the tension a little, then," the mercenary chief snarled.

Gesturing with an upraised arm and a circling hand, he brought his jeep to a halt as the other vehicle pulled up close. The men rapidly disembarked and checked their ordnance while Bolan marshaled them around him.

"You know what to do. Spread out, keep it real frosty and take position. Synchronize—" those men with watches joined him in so doing "—and in twenty you start maneuvers."

The men assented. Their game plan was simple. The arriving bidders had been perfectly timed—the Russians wouldn't be able to devote all their resources in coming to meet their attackers. Knowing that they were inside the cordon in two vehicles, they would be expecting a full-frontal assault.

They weren't going to get it. Make them wait, get nervous and anxious. Meantime, spread out and form a pincer. The enemy's greater numbers were neutralized by the need to secure and conduct the auction. Let that begin, perhaps— then attack.

But while they waited, Bolan had a preliminary of his own to undertake. Part reconnaissance and part expeditionary, he would go ahead of the pack and set up a few surprises of his own.

Bolan took a last look around the men who were serving with him, knowing it might be the last.

"We know what we need to do. Let's do it, and hope I see you all on the other side."

"GENTLEMEN, IF YOU will follow me, I will show you to where the auction is to take place. I would ask that your personal security keep their weapons out of sight and out of action. I will not insult you by asking them to discard these weapons, but remind you that this site has been secured by our men for your express safety and to expedite a quick, efficient and fair sale."

Piotr cast his eye over the throng that had disembarked from the choppers. Like animals from the ark, they came in pairs. The alpha males were the suited, briefcase-carrying men who exuded an air of authority; the lesser partners were the larger, security men with bulging armpits accompanying each alpha male, seemingly handpicked because they looked the part. Eyes hidden behind shades that were part functional, part shield and image, the security men were impassive, even when they looked around. The alpha male delegates, however, made no secret of the contempt and competition in their eyes as they sized each other up even before they followed the uniformed guards into the air-conditioned tent that had been prepared for them.

It was all show. They only wished to outgun each other with words and hard cash. Piotr only wished to get the sale concluded, ship the merchandise and then turn his attention to the matter of the American and his Arab men who had been dogging their footsteps.

His reverie was broken by the approach of the ex-general placed in charge of the camp.

"Please, this way," he murmured, taking Piotr's forearm to guide him toward the smaller tent that served as the Libyan's OP center. "Your friends are approaching. They have passed the outer defense line. I have sent a preliminary team to meet them. Look."

On his laptop, he clicked and replayed film from the cameras, showing the vehicles crossing the cordon of motion detectors and cameras. He played it at quarter speed so that Piotr had a good view of his approaching enemy. Data from the motion sensors played in sidebars, showing the weight of the vehicles, times crossed and speed.

"They don't give up, do they?" he muttered to himself. "But can they really be that careless?" He looked away from the laptop screen at the Libyan. "Thank you. Proceed as you think. I must inform my colleague."

This was something Vladimir would relish.

BOLAN COUNTED IN HIS head as he made his way across the sand toward the camp. The undulations of the desert gave him little cover, but he guessed that the bulk of the opposition forces would be directed either at the men he had left behind or maintaining security at the auction. He was also hoping for a wild-card entry from the UN planeload. They were inevitable, although their timing could not be relied upon.

As he progressed, he kept a weather eye on the small device he carried with him. If there were any other motion sensors or cameras, he would be able to skirt them. Nothing had shown so far, and he guessed that the need to set up the camp quickly had led them to use the tech purely as a cordoned warning system.

In desert camo, he was now within sight of the camp. Not that he could get a good view from his current position—a couple of vehicles and the blank canvas and tarp of some tenting were all that greeted him. There was also little in the way of any regular patrol. In fact, from this angle there was no sign of life at all.

As a survey it told him nothing. As a back-door entry, it was ideal. He made his way across the sands and into the outskirts of the camp.

Approaching, he could hear voices from several of the tents. In one, it sounded like one man on a communications system. Farther over he heard the babble of several voices, likely from the auction tent. By the sound of it, business had not yet commenced.

If that was the case, then his targets were not obscured by the mass of potential buyers. They were still contained somewhere. This would make them easier to take. But first he would have to locate them.

He carried the HK G3A4 slung across his back, with a .357 SIG P228 holstered on his thigh. But neither of these would be appropriate until the firefight began in earnest. He also had a benchmade Stryker automatic knife with a 4-inch Tanto blade, which he unsheathed as he moved toward the first tent in his path. A good piece of steel would be silent and more efficient.

Then he heard another sound that was barely audible beneath the voices. Distant, but getting closer.

Bolan allowed himself a small smile—his wild card was approaching.

PIOTR WAS ALMOST out of the tent when he heard the Libyan gasp. He turned back, looking over the shoulder of the ex-general at the laptop screen. The image of a large truck, played in real time, appeared.

"Who—" Piotr cut himself off. The question was irrelevant—the Libyan would know no more than he did. From the intel they had, the whole force that had followed them was concentrated in those two vehicles that had earlier crossed the cordon. This truck—with its unknown number of men—was an unknown quantity in all ways and could only be considered as hostile.

Perhaps Vladimir would not have the chance for revenge that he wished. Perhaps he would be too distracted by what was to come.

"They will be on top of us in no time. How many men do we have free?"

The Libyan looked at him, confused. "None. Why would we? I sent half out to deal with the enemy—the enemy we knew about," he corrected himself. "The rest are concentrated on the auction and guarding the merchandise."

Piotr stared at him. "We have no circulating guards?"

The Libyan shrugged. "I deployed as seemed appropriate."

Piotr swore softly in Russian. With that kind of sense, it was little wonder that the colonel's men had fallen so easily.

"Take them off the merchandise—just leave one. Take half off the auction tent—let those idiots try to blow each other away if they are that stupid. If we do not stop this, then whoever is incoming will do it for them."

Piotr hurried from the tent in search of his comrade, leaving the Libyan barking orders into the earpieces of the guards scattered between the camp and the desert beyond. He passed within a couple of yards of Bolan, who had been listening from his concealed position.

Bolan let the Russian go—time enough for him later. What he had heard suited him well. Spreading the confusion by taking out the Libyan and the communications center would be useful, but the timing was wrong. It would alert them too soon to an intruder right inside.

The merchandise—his target—was to be guarded by just the one man. Good. His job was to secure them and then set up a diversion. Not necessarily in that order.

Bolan moved on, leaving the Libyan to issue orders, unaware of how close he had come to his own death.

Bolan had to find the location where the scientists were being kept. If it was anything like the last encampment, they would be housed in a trailer until such time as they were brought before potential buyers. Moving between the layers of canvas, he heard footsteps approaching at the double and stepped back into cover as a guard ran past, muttering in Arabic into a mic.

Bolan's grin broadened—the guard had been taken off the merchandise. All he had to do was retrace the man's footsteps and he would have reached objective one.

A distant sound told him that it couldn't have been better timing.

HASSIM DIVIDED HIS men into four teams and sent them on their way. They would skirt the circumference of the camp, moving in as they did, so that they would be in position for the moment of attack. The signal for this would come from Cooper. If there was no signal by the designated time, then they would assume he was man down and proceed regardless.

But first, before Hassim, Shadeeb and Gamal would proceed, he had a little something for the guards to remember him by.

He had chosen Shadeeb to accompany him because the man was still less than fighting fit, and if anyone needed carrying, then Hassim—as leader—would do this. And Gamal was his protégé—the son he never had, as the cliché ran. But the orphan had been more or less adopted by the mercenary chief and his wife, and had shown himself to be a strong fighter even at his early age. Between them, Gamal and Hassim would cover any shortfall caused by Shadeeb's combat strains.

There was something else the boy was good at. While Hassim busied himself on one vehicle, and Shadeeb kept lookout, Gamal went to work on the other. Jared was happy to sacrifice the vehicles, since if they survived this firefight they could take their opponents' wheels. If they didn't survive, it hardly mattered anyway. Hassim and Gamal worked quickly, wiring up the vehicles to Claymore mines and Semtex. The detonators on each were wired up to receivers for motion detectors, which the two men rapidly placed just a couple of yards from the vehicles. Taking care to set them so that they had time to withdraw, the two men and their lookout then began their passage toward the encampment, being careful to keep out of sight as much as possible.

They could hear vehicles—one was at a ninety-degree angle to their location and seemed to be coming from the desert. Closer were two smaller vehicles. Motioning his men to take cover, Hassim watched as two jeeps sped out from the camp. As they approached the stationary vehicles he had just left, the two enemy jeeps pulled up, and after a short pause discharged their loads.

"Come on, just a little closer," Hassim breathed.

There were eight guards. They fanned out, their standard-issue BXP-10 SMGs leveled. They were uncertain, hesitant—

they had expected to meet a moving target head-on, and were instead faced with two deserted vehicles.

Don't get suspicious.... Not until it's too late, thought Hassim, hoping that they were just off guard enough to make a fatal...

Mistake—something that one of the guards realized just as one of his colleagues stepped forward. Perhaps it was the glimpse of something in the sand; perhaps it was that he had just figured out what he would do in these circumstances. Whatever it may have been, he yelled to the rest of the guards to hit the ground.

Not quickly enough for them to react. As the words left his mouth they were drowned by explosions triggered by the motion sensor. Both jeeps exploded simultaneously, the Semtex in them causing body parts to spray out with the heat and flame.

More damaging were the Claymore mines that they had planted with the explosives. Shrapnel and ball bearings shot out from the charges, spraying the immediate area with molten metal at high speed. The action of the mines caused a spread of metal that left no escape. Not a single one of the guards, no matter what kind of evasive action they took, could avoid the deadly load.

Hassim put his head down into the sand, covering it with one arm while pressing Gamal's head into the sand with the other. For one panicked second, as sand rained down on them, he wondered if they had actually distanced themselves enough.

Only sand—there was no metal to pierce their flesh, and when he looked up the sight before him was like a charnel house. All eight of the enemy were down, and their vehicle was reduced to a smoking wreck. The men lay at unnatural angles across the sand, blackened and bloodied, torn by the shrapnel and ball bearings. It was unlikely that any of them could have survived, but caution was a necessity. Hassim scrambled to his feet and motioned to his two men to follow.

Quickly they scanned the eight prone guards. Six were dead. Two were breathing. It took a tap on his MP5 in the face of each to end their suffering.

He looked at his watch. "Time is tight. Let's get moving."

VLADIMIR WAS IN the auction tent. He sized up the men before him. Soft. And that was just the bodyguards. He wouldn't have given them five minutes in a real firefight. Piotr had allowed the Libyan to allot too many of their meager forces to these idiots. They may be needed elsewhere.

That thought was only reinforced by the sound of an explosion—no, two, close together—in the desert. The babble in the tent increased immediately, the delegates looking nervous, the bodyguards looking tense, trying to seem cool but betraying their nerves by the way their hands twitched uselessly for their weapons.

"Gentlemen, please," Vladimir said. There was no pleading in his tone—rather, it was icy and commanding, his voice cutting through the hubbub.

"What is going on? We are supposed to be having a secured meeting," one of the bidders shouted, rising to his feet. He was Jordanian, and Vladimir reflected that the man was possibly more nervous because he would have preferred the sale to have gone ahead in his own land.

"We *are* having a secured meeting," Vladimir returned. He gestured for the man to be seated, indicating with a flicker of the eye for one of his men to cover the Jordanian's increasingly jumpy bodyguard. "The fact that there is some attempt at intrusion is only to be expected. That is why we have a secured zone. That is why you hear our men eliminating the threat. Now, if you will…"

He had no idea if that last statement was accurate. He

hoped so. He needed to get out of the auction tent and see what was happening. He was relieved to see Piotr appear at the far end of the tent.

He was, until he caught his partner's expression.

13

Bolan waited. The confusion surrounding the explosion gave him just the cover he needed. He would have preferred to lay down his distractions first, but that could wait. There was, from what he had overheard, now just the one guard in the trailer that stood before him.

Checking that it was clear before he broke cover, he made the distance to the trailer door in a couple of strides. Figuring that the door was probably unlocked, he tried it. It yielded easily to the touch, and he flung it open.

In one glance he took in the interior of the trailer. To the left of the door, standing toward the rear, were two men in suits. Both looked beaten and cowed, and stood mouth agape at the sudden movements. No threat there. The right-hand side of the trailer was another matter. An Arab guard stood, half turned toward the noise of the opening door, SMG pointing down but moving up as Bolan took a stride into the trailer interior.

The Arab was closer to the door than the two men in suits. His half-turned stance left him with legs spread. Bolan took advantage of this by taking his next stride and bringing up his heavy desert boot so that it caught the man square in the crotch.

The shock took the breath from him, the guard's mouth forming a silent *O* as wide as his eyes. He bent forward involuntarily, and Bolan followed his movement through to make the most of this, grasping the man by the back of the neck and thrusting him down to the floor. The guard's face was ground into the floor as Bolan lifted the Stryker. Shifting his grip so that it was on the man's hair he tugged it back, bringing his neck into view.

Before the guard had a chance to scream—either in fear or in warning—the sound bubbled in his throat, drowned by the blood as Bolan sliced across the throat. Blood spurted briefly before the jet was stifled as Bolan thrust the guard's face down into the floor once more, counting as the life seeped out of his enemy.

He stood after wiping the knife on the dead guard's uniform. The two suited men were staring at him. One of them, the older one, looked like he was going to burst into tears.

"No time to explain. I'm here to get you out and back to the U.S.A., then you'll be returned to your own land. Follow me."

He turned to leave, but halted when he saw that they were frozen to the spot. They had been through an ordeal, but this was not the time for sympathy.

"Now! Unless you want to die here," he snapped, beckoning them.

Almost reluctantly, they followed him out. First thing he would have to do was find them cover until the firefight was done. Pity. The trailer would have been ideal if not for the fact that it was the first place any enemies would look for them. Cursing this, an idea suddenly came to Bolan. It seemed crazy, and under any other circumstances, it would have seemed funny, but it might just work.

He beckoned the two men to follow him as he wound back the way he had come. The Stryker was holstered again and the HK G3A4 was off his shoulder and ready to fire. He didn't want to use it yet, as he figured his compatriots were still closing on the camp, and he was heavily outnumbered. But if he was spotted, close hand-to-hand would not be an option. Circumstances wouldn't leave him much choice. He could only hope that his luck held. With the panic that was now starting to take hold in the camp, he expected to see at least one guard stumble blindly into them as they made the short distance to the OP tent.

Bolan felt like someone wanted him to complete this one—they made it without sight of anyone. Considering he was carrying these two traumatized passengers, it was nothing short of a miracle. He pulled back the flap of the tent and stepped in. The Libyan was sitting with his back to the flap, leaning over his laptop. He was wearing a headset but was not speaking. He was so absorbed that he did not notice Bolan's silent entry. Bolan checked his watch—only a couple of minutes. The risk was that the Libyan's absence would be noted before the attack began in earnest. This would leave the targets exposed.

But he had no time to waste. He hadn't as yet laid down the diversions, and this needed his immediate attention. He would have to take the chance.

Stepping forward, he shouldered the HK G3A4 and took his knife from its sheath. Still, the Libyan, absorbed in his task, did not hear him. It was only at the last footfall that he began to turn—too late to help himself as Bolan grasped him firmly with one arm in a headlock and slicing his throat.

The two scientists had followed him in to the tent, and seemed either too hardened or too traumatized to take notice of the bloodied corpse slumped on the groundsheet.

Bolan took the Libyan's pistol—a Desert Eagle .357, once much favored by himself and a common handgun in this region—and handed it to the younger scientist, who seemed to be the more together of the two.

"You know how to use this?" he asked. The young man

shook his head, and Bolan gave him a twenty-second crash course in handling a weapon. "Stay here, and only use this if you have to. I'll be back," he finished, feeling uneasy at leaving the two men alone. However, he had other urgent matters that needed his attention.

Bolan carried C-4 and Semtex with detonators—small charges, so that they would cause disruption but not collateral damage and threaten the targets. Moving swiftly around the compound, he laid charges on a ninety-second timer before returning to the OP tent. As he entered, Gabriel leveled the Desert Eagle at him. For a moment, Bolan thought panic might make him jerk off a shot. Chances were it would miss, but it was more the attention it would draw to the OP tent than any risk to his own safety that concerned the soldier.

Gabriel let out a sigh of relief and held the Desert Eagle downward. He was about to say something when he was cut short by the first of the charges going off.

"Showtime," Bolan told him with a grin.

HASSIM, GAMAL AND SHADEEB were in cover, half buried in a sand dune, when the charges detonated. Hassim had been listening to the approaching truck. From where he was, it was out of sight. But it sounded big. He wondered how many extra men they would have to take on.

No matter. Bolan was alive, and he had laid the diversionary charges. Hassim was on his feet and running toward the camp before the echo had died in his ears, his men at his back. He knew that, from their respective points around the circumference, the rest of his men would also be on their way.

IT TOOK VLADIMIR some time to reassure the bidders that they were safe. Then, seeing his compatriot's grim mien, he had rapidly made excuses and left the auction tent. Outside,

Piotr began to tell him about the truck that had breached their sensors.

"Never mind that shit, what were the explosions? Our men taking out those ass pains or—"

"I don't know. I was out of the OP before they went off. But never mind that. This new intrusion—"

He was cut off by the first of the diversionary charges as it went off on the far side of the camp. Before either man had a chance to react, another charge went off.

"Shit— They're in here?" Piotr asked.

Vladimir pulled his Beretta 93R from its clamshell holster in the small of his back. "Some of them, all of them, I don't care. I'm sick of them fucking with us," he snarled and stormed off through the compound, Piotr watching him as guards rushed seemingly without aim across the gaps between the tents.

BOLAN LEFT THE two scientists in the OP tent once more. He was uneasy about leaving them, but in truth there was too much to be done before his men swooped down on the compound. They would still run the risk of being outnumbered when the other force arrived. Anything he could do to even the odds would help.

Since the charges had gone off successfully, there was no need for subterfuge; he racked the HK G3A4 as he strode between the tents—there were two others beside the OP and the auction tent, which was by far the largest. Taking care to keep himself hidden for as long as possible, he surveilled both tents. One had served as a dorm tent for the guards who were off watch, and was empty. The second carried the camp's ordnance, and Bolan could see that they were carrying a firearms rather than rocket or grenade armory. It was light, and designed purely for a twenty-four to forty-eight hour stay. There was nothing here that he could use against them.

He paused. Ordnance was not the only thing in the tent. There were two tarps wrapping cylindrical shapes. He knew what was in them even before he stooped to look. Pulling back the tops of the rolled tarps, he saw that one held Rafik's corpse, the other that of Aref. He had not known them long, but Rafik in particular had been a good man, a good soldier. Hassim's boys would want blood for this. Bolan, his face set hard, knew how they felt.

Covering the faces of both men as he stood up, he shook the feeling from him—it would serve no purpose.

He stepped out into the camp once more. Two tents empty. Another with the targets, and one more containing the auction bidders. Everything else was in the open. That should even the odds. How many of the enemy, he wondered, were occupied with the parties in the auction tent?

"GENTLEMEN, I WOULD ask you to take your seats." Piotr's voice rang out over the clashing voices of the panicked throng. The bidders rose from their seats, their security men facing off against each other as they jostled for the exit, ignoring Piotr. There was no thought of the sale anymore—only getting out of a disintegrating situation as quickly as possible.

Piotr sighed and gestured to the guards at the tent flap. There were two on each side.

One of the guards leveled his BXP-10 at the crowded interior, while the other raised his to the ceiling of the tent and ripped through the canvas with a short burst designed to focus the attention of the crowd.

The babble of voices died away, the bidders silenced, shocked and also scared that they would be treated this way.

"That is much better. You will be safer in here." Piotr

spoke calmly, trying not to think of his paymaster's response to this tactic. "For your own security, we ask you to stay calm and seated while our men on the outside deal with this small problem."

At least, he hoped it would prove to be small.

GUARDS FROM THE CAMP met the oncoming truck as it jarred and bumped over the sands. Falling into defensive positions they opened up with their BXP 10's, the SMG fire shattering the windshield and causing the truck to veer sideways on the sand, slipping down the incline of a dune so that the men in the rear were thrown across the interior.

This just served to make them mad. Responding to the yelled orders of their sergeant, the Marines disembarked and took up positions of their own in the sand, responding to the offensive fire with shots of their own. They were also better armed—expecting much more of a firefight—than the hired security. A couple of grenades spread shrapnel among the guards, killing two and maiming three others, putting them out of effective action. A blanket of CS or KooKol-1 would have been a usual procedure for securing target personnel in this situation, as the Marines were armed with breathing apparatus, but the open conditions reduced any effectiveness. The only thing to do now was go in, and go in hard.

The guards who were left standing began to move back toward the camp, in search of cover and backup. They laid down suppressing fire that pinned the Marines into the cover they had made for themselves, but did not claim any casualties, and those guards who were able to pull back had a feeling already that this was a losing battle.

As they attained their cover, the Marines started to form up and split into groups that would spread and attack in a pincer movement.

They were proving to be just the diversion that Bolan

would have wanted for his men, but at the same time they had the same target.

This could prove problematic.

THOSE GUARDS LEFT in camp and not assigned to the auction tent were unprepared for the attack from Hassim's forces. The diversionary charges—large enough to cause a big bang but too small to cause any real damage—had taken them by surprise, and their reaction had not been that of disciplined men. It didn't help that they had nothing coming through their headsets, and so were unaware of what was going on around them.

They didn't expect the Arab mercenaries to come from many directions. Hassim's men were experienced desert fighters and had kept themselves low and under the radar as they advanced, until they were on top of the camp itself. It was only then that they rose up and attacked in force.

Their first-wave assault took the mercenaries into the heart of the camp. The guards were uniformed, making them easy to pick out, so several of them fell immediately to efficient taps of three-shot bursts. The Arabs were as much concerned with finding their missing compatriots as they were with locating Bolan's targets; their fury at longtime comrades being taken had obscured the paid objective.

It was Haithem who found the two corpses in the ordnance tent. His cries brought Hassim to the enclosure. Outside, the remaining guards had fallen into defensive positions, and had entrenched themselves in the auction tent, which was surrounded.

Hassim spat on the floor in disgust as Haithem unrolled both tarps to reveal the extent of the torture on their compatriots.

"They will be avenged," he said with a snarl. "This place—we raze it. All these fuckers die."

"What about Cooper and his two men?" Haithem asked.

Hassim shook his head. "We let him take them—they are victims like our men. But no matter what he says, everyone else dies. Yes?"

He looked down on his friends. He had grown up in the same village as Aref, had known him all his life.

"All of them," he said softly.

VLADIMIR HAD TRIED to impose some kind of order on the chaos. He had seen the first of the invaders and snapped off a couple of shots before a volley of fire had forced him back. The guards had rushed around in panic and confusion—and had no idea of how to fight back. He had caught one of them, hit him hard across the face and yelled at him to shape up, get a team together and form a defensive ring. The man had just looked at him as if he was insane and babbled something about having no idea of what was happening as there was no voice in his ear.

Vladimir cursed and turned the man loose. The idiot Libyan ex-general must have panicked. Vladimir felt as though he was working with amateurs and cowards. He made his way toward the OP tent. If the Libyan was there, he would have words with him—at the very least. If Vladimir was not, then he would try and establish some kind of order before hunting down the dog and putting him to a deserved death.

The Berretta in hand as he strode through the tent flap, he froze in his tracks as he came face-to-face with Gabriel and Hoeness. The older man was still cowering, his nerves shot. The younger man looked scared, but there was a determination about him.

More importantly, Vladimir's attention was taken by the Desert Eagle in the scientist's grip. His hand was trembling, but not enough to ensure that he would miss.

The primary mission was still in the Russian's mind, and

he was loath to shoot down the scientist unless it was a matter of life for life.

It was then that he noticed the dead body of the Libyan on the groundsheet.

"Well, well," he said calmly, bringing up his own pistol so that it was leveled at the scientist. "Perhaps you have more guts than I gave you credit for. Question is, can you do it again? And would it be wise to try?"

14

Osterman had an apartment that served as his home when he was in Washington. It was functional rather than luxurious. Living room, bedroom, bathroom, kitchen—that was all. It was in a brownstone block twenty minutes' drive from his office. His normal routine was rise early, pound the pavement for thirty minutes to warm up for the day and follow this with a shower, coffee, juice and bran before hitting the office. It was a healthy lifestyle, a regular routine, and just lately that was all that had been keeping Osterman sane.

This morning was different. He rose sluggishly, having hardly slept, and didn't bother to take his run. He showered, hoping to wash off the fog of torpor, and did without all except the coffee, which was black and piping hot, to try and stir his brain cells.

No matter what, he kept coming around to the same thing—there was no way he could keep sending a detachment of Marines into Libya under wraps. Equally, there was no way he could prove who had put him under pressure to do this. No way, either, that he could save his career. He was screwed.

He had no idea that fate was about to step in and hand him a Get Out of Jail Free card.

Preoccupied as he was, he didn't hear the lock on his front door softly click. Neither did he hear the entry of the man whose appearance in the kitchen, seemingly out of nowhere, made him start.

"Who the fu—" Osterman reached for his gun as he spoke, halting when he realized that he was not wearing the weapon—another consequence of his distraction.

"That would not have been a good idea, Colonel," the tall, heavy-set man standing over him said softly. He held a SIG-Sauer P229 in one hand, and a dossier in the other. He laid the dossier down on the kitchen work surface. Osterman looked at the folder, then up at the man who loomed over him. There was something familiar about him.

"I know you, don't I?" Osterman said with an air of resignation.

"Not personally. I don't believe we've ever actually been introduced. But you've probably seen me around. I'd be very surprised if you hadn't. I've certainly seen you. Although I have to say, I didn't know much about you until recently. Very recently."

Osterman's eyes went back to the dossier. "It doesn't look that way," he said mildly.

"It's surprising how quickly you can pull information together when you have a real need," the stranger said. "All you need are a couple of threads, and then it all kind of comes together of its own accord."

Osterman's mouth puckered. "It's never that simple, is it?"

"No, maybe not. You're a smart man, Colonel. It's not entirely your fault that circumstances got the better of you. Blackmail is an ugly word, but it's possible that in doing your duty, and in defence of your country, you found yourself painted into a corner where whatever action you took would compromise you in some way. If that were the case, then it could also be true that someone may be able to use that unwitting compromise to gain leverage on you." The stranger sighed. "The trouble with that kind of action is that it never ends there, does it? Leverage leads to further compromise, which leads to further leverage, and so forth. It becomes a spiral that could go on ad infinitum."

"You, of course, being part of that process," Osterman said softly. "I do recognize you. I was made aware of you again only recently, as I'm sure you could tell me. As I'm sure is in here," he added, placing his hand on the dossier. "You're Brognola, and it's your turn to put the pressure on me," he added in a resigned tone.

"Yes and no," Brognola replied with a shrug. "I *am* putting pressure on you—hell, breaking into your apartment first thing in the morning and keeping a gun on you could hardly be construed as anything else. But I can end the spiral. I only want one thing from you."

"That is what they all say," Osterman said wryly. "It always begins that way."

"Of course," Brognola replied. "But this really is about the one thing. That UN flight you sanctioned. It had a detachment of Marines on it. I know where they are going, and I know why. And I want them pulled out. Now."

Osterman looked at the clock on the kitchen wall. "Local time? I'd say it was too late. They should already be in position, if not in action."

"Even if they are, I want the mission aborted. I want them out of there, so my man can fulfill his mission."

"Man?" Osterman looked up, surprised. For a moment he had forgotten his own situation. "You have just one man in there?"

Brognola smiled. "He's got a little local help, but yeah—just the one man." He caught the expression on Osterman's face. "If you knew him, you'd understand." He grinned. "Now listen, Colonel. In this dossier we have full documentation of your involvement, and evidence to back up not only your coercion, but also that you were acting on behalf of my department as a mole, and that your depth of involvement is down to your service—on my behalf, again—to your country. I also have honorable discharge papers that bring your retirement forward to tomorrow. You've still got work to do today, providing you agree and that you sign on the dotted."

"What about Chronos?"

"You let me worry about that."

"And Senator—"

Brognola cut him off. "The senator won't be causing anyone any problems after today, Colonel."

Osterman looked Brognola in the eye. He nodded, and held out his hand. "Give me a pen," he said. "Then hand me that phone." He indicated his phone, in the living room. "It's a secure line."

"I know it is," Brognola said flatly as he watched Osterman sign. "Now call," he added, handing the Colonel his own cell.

BOLAN HAD BEEN caught in the middle of the initial firefight, pinned down as guards rushed to meet the oncoming Arabs. He had taken out one man who had come too close, using the Stryker once more as he did not wish to bring the whole weight of the camp upon him. The sounds of their clashes were deafeningly loud around him as he tried to keep out of sight, moving back toward the OP tent.

Hassim and his men were fulfilling their function well. He could identify the fire as it rang out, and the sound of the Russian-made BXP 10, almost identical to the MAC-10 it copied, was erratic in frequency and timing while the bursts of fire from the assorted SMGs and assault rifles of the Arabs was more assured and regular.

He knew that he could trust Hassim's men to clean up the guards while he returned and secured both the targets and also a means of getting them off location. The latter was becoming more urgent, as he could hear the sounds of a fire-fight between the other attacking force and the detachment of guards sent to face them.

It was getting closer, and from the sound of it, the camp guards were not faring too well in that battle, either. Ideally, he wanted to get the targets and get out just ahead of the fresher, possibly larger force on the approach.

Ideally.

As he reached the OP tent he knew that it was not going to be that easy. Even with the sounds of battle around him, he was close enough to hear voices from within the tent. Close enough to hear that one of them was Russian.

Cursing under his breath, his stealth carried him unde-tected to the threshold of the OP. He was able to peer through the semi-open tent flap and take in the scene. The older scientist was cowering near the back of the tent, while the younger one had the Desert Eagle raised, trembling, against an armed man who was speaking to him. One who had his own weapon—a pistol, though Bolan could not identify it from this angle—leveled on the young scientist.

The tall, shaven-headed Russian was undoubtedly the man he had seen on the Syrian gunboat. He was speaking in a heavily accented, but level voice.

"If you stop this idiocy and hand me that gun, I will not have to shoot you. You have not the skill or the nerve to shoot me, my friend. If I, on the other hand, shoot you, it will be in the gut. Have you ever seen anyone shot that way? No, probably not. It is a very slow and painful way to die. I would leave you here, and by the time your saviors find you, presuming they defeat us, it will be too late for them to save you. If you come with me, however, you will live. Those who are our paymasters will think we have perished with the rest, and you will be able to go free."

He was smart. Bolan had to give him that. As irrational

as it sounded—indeed, as irrational as it was—in his traumatized state the young scientist almost believed it. His arm began to drop. Simultaneously, the Russian's shoulder tightened as he began to squeeze the trigger on his own pistol.

Shooting him would not deflect his aim, but Bolan was only a couple of yards from him. He leapt across the distance, his momentum carrying the Russian with him as he careened into his back. The Beretta barked, its discharge flying at an angle through the roof of the tent.

Bolan and Vladimir grappled on the ground. Bolan's fingers sought pressure points to black out his enemy as he rolled beneath him. The Russian dropped his weapon, preferring to rely on his own hands in close. He countered as they rolled, Bolan now on top, by attempting to pry the soldier's hands loose, slipping his arms under Bolan's in order to force them apart. At the same time he brought his knee up and into the soldier's groin.

A sharp pain shot through Bolan's groin and thigh, although he twisted to avoid the worst of the impact. In so doing, he relaxed his grip and rolled away from the Russian, propelling himself to his feet and unsheathing the Stryker as he did so. Vladimir scrambled toward his Beretta, allowing Bolan the chance to kick him in the ribs, the heavy desert combat boot driving the air from Vladimir's lungs and knocking him sideways. As he rolled, Bolan was on him, forcing him onto his front with a knee in his back to pin him down before lifting him under the chin and delivering the final blow with the Tanto steel blade.

Breathing heavily, he rose to his feet, checking as he did that the two scientists were still in the tent. They were standing, watching, dumbstruck. Bolan figured that the Russian had decided to cut his losses. There was no doubt that he had intended to kill them, regardless of his orders. The man had gone rogue.

As for these two, he thought as he looked at them, let's just hope it's worth getting them out of here; at this moment they looked like they wouldn't be much use to anyone. In fact, it might just be an achievement to actually get them out without their sanity snapping.

"Come on," he barked. "Forget him. You want to get out alive? Follow me and do what I say."

He led them out of the OP tent and into the fray beyond.

THE MARINES HAD taken up offensive positions and were steadily advancing on the camp. The guards that had been sent out to meet them had started the firefight, but were unable to stand up to the onslaught that they had unleashed. The Marine force included better tactical thinkers, had greater firepower and in terms of numbers also had an advantage. Although the Marines had been in the open and thus at an initial disadvantage, it had been only a matter of seconds before they were able to make their superiority felt.

Driving the guards back toward the cover of the camp, the Marines fanned out and kept up a covering fire that allowed them to advance in twos while pinning down their enemy. The guards either had to risk their cover in order to fall back or be overtaken. Left with little option other than to retreat, they were being picked off, their numbers slowly decreasing as they moved back. And while the guards were yelling into their headsets, receiving no orders, no intel and no feedback from their OP, the Marines were in constant communication through their headsets, handing them yet another advantage.

Before the guards had any real opportunity to take stock of what was happening to them, they found that half their number had been taken out by the stream of suppressing fire, while the rest found themselves retreating into a camp that was in itself a hostile fire zone.

HASSIM DIRECTED HIS men without the need for comms; the group had fought together too often, knew each other too well to need anything other than the barest of orders. They were men who knew not only how to fight in confined areas, but also how the others thought as much as fought. Using the narrow spaces between the tents as corridors of death, they stalked their opponents, taking cover in the folds of the canvas and the dark spaces between before stepping into the open to deliver short taps of death that gradually ate into the numbers of their opponents.

It was not a full-fledged firefight like the one that was taking place out on the sands beyond the camp, but was no less debilitating to the opposition. Not, however, one that left Hassim's men without casualties. Amin and Abd, the young brothers in blood if not by birth who watched each other's backs throughout the combat, were caught out by a guard who, frozen with terror, was lurking near the area where the three Hueys were berthed. The two Arab fighters had been detailed to secure the choppers, whose crews were still with them and had remained within their confines, hoping to avoid the fray. The crews had been hired to fly, not fight, and had every intention of sitting this one out.

Hassim had other ideas. One of the three choppers would be the route by which he would ship his men—perhaps Cooper and his targets, if they were alive—out of the area, so he sent the two fighters to flush out the crews.

The two Arabs had taken cover on the edge of the berthing area, and had started to tap out short bursts designed to drive the crews into the open. They did not want to substantially damage the choppers, so their blasts were carefully aimed at taking out the ports and creating an environment inside that the crews would not wish to stay within.

It seemed to work at first; there was no initial return of fire, and the Arabs stayed in cover as the crews reluctantly vacated their crafts, taking whatever cover they could find in order to return fire. Their shooting was that of pilots rather than hardened fighters, and with careful taps the two Arab fighters were able to pick off four out of the six crewmen, driving the remaining two back toward the sand dunes on the edge of the camp area. As Amin and Abd advanced, one covering the other as each moved in formation, the lurking guard was able to emerge from the cover in which he had cowered, picking them off. It was little consolation that the one-eyed Haithem avenged their death by taking out the guard. He spat on the corpse of the guard, cursing his late arrival on the scene, before taking out the remaining two chopper crew members, who used the cutting down of their attackers to try and get back to their machines.

The Hueys were now free and fair game for anyone who could fly them. Haithem and Hassim knew that they had the skills in their group. Could any of those left out of the opposition force say the same?

This force was reduced to the few guards who were left in the auction tent and the delegates and bodyguards who had arrived for the auction that had been so drastically terminated.

The Arabs had left this tent alone, content to lay down a suppressing fire that confined the parties within the canvas. With only one obvious point of exit, Hassim stationed Shadeeb at the front, in cover, with orders for the fighter to blast the hell out of anyone who poked their head or gun out, and if they tried to break to just use his RPG-7 and blow them out of the desert. The older Arab had looked askance at his leader when told this; any kind of shrapnel grenade at this close range and in a confined camp risked collateral damage to his own men. But seeing the light of hate and anger in Hassim's eyes, and knowing what this kind of mood engendered, he merely agreed while deciding to put his trust in his 5.56 mm M4 carbine.

Bolan came across Hassim as they mopped up the last of the guards who were not in the tent. The two scientists were with him, and Hassim indicated them.

"Got the boys, eh? Time for us to make for the border, I think."

"Not quite," Bolan said. "We've still got a tent full of potential trouble, and I think there's more on the way."

The chatter of SMG fire as the Marines hit the edge of the camp only served to emphasize his words.

"Why don't any of these fuckers ever give up?" Hassim sighed.

15

Piotr stepped back from the flap of the tent as fire from the M4 carbine raked past him and across the inside of the tent. Pandemonium reigned as the assembled bidders panicked, and their bodyguards sought to protect them. Bodies blocked each other and tumbled into tangled limbs, chairs scattering and adding to the confusion as people sought to avoid being hit.

Piotr swore loudly, and indicated to his men to stand back around the edges of the crowd and keep clear of the tangle. He realized that to shout and try to restore order would be pointless in the chaos and the noise of the firefight outside. Indicating with gestures, he sought to marshal his men toward the rear of the tent. They could not use the front, but from the sound of fire outside, he doubted that the enemy could spare the manpower to cover the rear. The tent was thick canvas and tarp, reinforced by steel poles, and would be difficult to cut through quickly and without drawing attention to the action. But it was their best bet, as there was little chance of sighting the man covering the front without sparking another burst into the interior and causing more panic.

At this time, he didn't give a crap about the so-called powerful men in the tent. His only concern was to get his own ass—and those of his men, if possible—out of this death trap and into a position where they could escape. He wondered if Vladimir was in the same position elsewhere, or if he had already succumbed to the Berserker instincts that Piotr had always feared would claim him.

"Knife, blade, anything," he yelled at his men, snapping his fingers. One of the men thrust a Tekna into his hand, and he started to methodically hack at the canvas, hoping he had time, and that no one would be waiting for him on the other side.

Two of the bodyguards—an American and a Ukrainian— left their charges and broke away from the crowd and came toward him.

"Hey, what are you doing?" the American said, a SIG Sauer P229 in his fist.

Piotr sighed, stopped cutting and drew his own pistol. "Every man for himself, my friend," he said, tapping a clean shot into the American's face. The Ukrainian reacted, but too slow. As he leveled his own gun, two shots from Piotr took him out, the first was off target and tore a chunk from his throat, leaving the artery spurting. The second shot tapped him the forehead, making certain.

Oddly, no one else seemed to notice the confrontation in the confusion, so the Russian returned to his task, directing his men to cover him.

"GAMAL, TAKE THESE two and keep them safe. We want to use the choppers. Take them to Haithem and then pick up Shadeeb. Screw those bastards in the tent, we need to haul our asses out of here now," Hassim shouted at his young protégé, manhandling the two scientists and shoving them toward the young man.

"Go with him, it's safer," Bolan ordered the two scientists as they hesitated. They were traumatized, sure, but if he was going to save their hides this was no time for niceties.

As the young man hauled them out of the immediate line

of fire, Bolan turned to Hassim. The Arab mercenary leader now had Sami and Husni with him, while four others were going up against the Marines. The other half of Hassim's men were dead.

With the guards who had opposed them now wiped out, the Marines advanced rapidly toward the four mercenaries as they took covering positions and started to open fire. They had little chance of making any real impact, but were determined to stop the advance long enough for Gamal to gather his comrade and the targets, and get them to where the one-eyed mercenary was ready to take flight. Hassim knew that Haithem could fly a chopper, and he had some knowledge himself. He had no doubt that Cooper could do this, too. They only needed one chopper for their group's survivors.

Question was, could they hold the Marines at bay long enough to get to a Huey?

The Marine detachment outnumbered them by at least three to one, and the mercenaries were driven back by the waves of fire. Their initial bursts of suppression turned into desperate shots designed to try and hold the Americans at bay. It felt wrong to Bolan to be doing this, firing on his own countrymen, but in this moment they were his enemies, guided as they were by a rogue element, however unwittingly.

Sami yelled in pain as he was hit in the thigh, his M4 firing wildly as he fell back.

Their only option was to grab the wounded man and make a desperate fallback. Hassim went to gather his comrade while Husni and Bolan formed up to cover them.

And then the strangest thing happened. The Marines ceased firing, and the only sounds were suddenly the intermittent bursts from Bolan and Husni. These stopped quickly when they realized that the Marines had not only ceased fire, but were now pulling back.

Bolan had no idea why this was happening, but was in no mood to hang around and question his luck. He figured some guardian angel was looking out for him, not imagining that it took the shape of the big Fed, Hal Brognola.

For the briefest moment, the four men stood still, frozen in surprise at what was happening. Bolan was the first to move, his reflexes and instincts not allowing him to stand still.

"C'mon, let's go," he snapped, helping Hassim to shoulder the injured man. "Keep us covered," he told Husni.

They moved swiftly across camp to the area where the Hueys were waiting. Gamal, Haithem and Shadeeb had the area covered from one of the choppers and were visibly relieved when the four men appeared. Bolan could see the scientists within the Huey.

"Help him," Hassim ordered, handing Sami over to the oncoming Gamal, Husni having already taken weight from Bolan. The mercenary leader turned to the soldier.

"What do we do about those bastards in the tent?"

Bolan grinned mercilessly. "Just keep me covered. They'll be on us in a moment, if I'm not wrong." There were cries and shouts, and the odd gunshot emanating from the area of the auction tent. It was obvious that there was dissension inside, as they had also realized that they were no longer pinned down.

While Hassim took cover and trained his SMG on the area directly in front of the choppers, Bolan set to work disabling the two remaining Hueys. It wasn't subtle sabotage, but it would ensure that the helicopters were no longer in any condition to fly. He placed a Claymore mine in each, ensuring that whoever took the first step into the chopper would render it not airworthy while also putting themselves out of the game.

It took him only a couple of minutes, though it seemed like hours as he carefully set the mines before running across to

the remaining Huey where Gamal had taken over cover from
Hassim, who was now beside Haithem, preparing for takeoff.

"Go," Bolan yelled as he came aboard, moving past the
youth who remained in position at the open hatch of the chopper, ready to cover them as they ascended.

"Not a moment too soon," he added to himself as the
Huey took to the air.

PIOTR WAS STILL hacking at the canvas when he heard the
firefight outside suddenly die down. He stopped, puzzled.
The faces of his men showed the same confusion. An air of
hesitancy and tension lay like a fog over the others in the
tent as they wondered if this meant they would be saved or
slaughtered. A few seconds yielded neither result, and their
hesitancy was broken as Piotr and his guard cleaved through
them. Snapping orders, Piotr directed two of his men to
lay down a covering fire through the flap while he looked
around. It was a huge risk, but he was already convinced that
there would be no one there.

He didn't understand what had just happened, but he was
pretty sure that it had been some kind of withdrawal. In
which case, then, surely anyone left would attack the last
remaining enclave—the auction tent?

That hadn't happened. Had both enemy forces withdrawn?
If so, it was his cue to get his men the hell out. This had gone
from a discreet auction with a few blind eyes paid for, to a
full-scale firefight in the oasis region. There was no way it
would go unnoticed. Even if unwillingly, the National Transitional Council would be forced to send at least a token force
to investigate and mop up.

Piotr had no intention of hanging around waiting for those
awkward questions.

The Syrian delegate grabbed him as he passed. He had
time to blurt out, "What about us? You can't leave us—" be-

fore one of the guards bludgeoned him down, another firing into the face of the bodyguard who sought to protect his charge. Unrest bubbled in the tent as the delegates realized that they were to be left to their own fate. Similarly, their bodyguards began to think about carving a way out, realizing that the space was so tight that any kind of firefight would cause problems and endanger their own charges.

Piotr was out of the tent, his men following swiftly with a rearguard action as the dissent grew, with random bursts of weapons fire testifying to the panic within.

Piotr swore heavily as his team reached the edge of the camp, only to be pinned back by a burst of fire from the Huey that was rising into the sky. His men returned fire as the chopper spun in the sky, the Arab crew rusty and familiarizing themselves with the controls. Ironically, it made them harder to hit, and although the covering fire from the chopper was erratic because of this, it made it harder to access the two remaining choppers.

Piotr zigzagged his way across the sand, hoping that the combination of cover from his men and the spinning trajectory of the Huey would make it less likely that he could be picked out, and that his luck would hold just long enough to reach one of the helicopters.

Blowing hard, he ran through the hatch into the Huey, thanking God or whoever had landed him in this forsaken hole that he had flown choppers in his time. All he needed to do was get the damned thing going, then his men could load up and he could join those other bastards in the skies. Screw anyone else.

He looked back briefly to see that his men were advancing, covering their rear and now relatively safe from fire from above as the first Huey had risen out of effective range.

It was his fatal error. He did not see the Claymore and its detonator until his foot was almost on it. He screamed, more from frustration than fear, as he knew that his muscle reaction would be too slow to halt his foot from landing on the mine.

So close.

"WHOA," JARED EXCLAIMED as the concussion from below bucked the Huey, even at the height it had attained. They were high enough for him and Haithem to wrest back control easily as they looked down on the carnage.

Below them, the blast from the first Huey had spread shrapnel and debris that had triggered the Claymore in the second chopper. Both were now smoking, flaming ruins, the shrapnel and blast damage also having laid waste to most of the remaining guard force that had been following Piotr to the first chopper. Driven back into the camp, the men in the airborne Huey could see the auction delegates and their bodyguards milling in the camp, those not injured or killed by the blast wandering in shock and wondering how the hell they were going to get away before the inevitable arrival of native forces.

"They'll have a lot of explaining to do." Haithem chuckled.

Bolan's face wrinkled in a grimace. "Sad to say, but I doubt that they'll actually have to do too much. Those that survive the NTC blundering in will have too much influence to do anything other than get away scot-free. But at least they didn't get what they were after," he added, looking back into the chopper at the two scientists.

Hassim spat in disgust. "Six men for them. It doesn't seem worth it."

"It's the price, my friend. You took the pay."

"I know," the Arab replied softly, leaving the rest unsaid.

16

Bolan stood looking at the memorial. So many names. When his time came, he doubted that he would appear on such a monument. It didn't matter, really—only in that he could look at it and ponder how many unknown and unrecorded there were for each fallen man who made the cut?

"It's a lot of men. Could have been a few more out there." Brognola's voice was soft at his shoulder. Bolan turned to face him, and the two men proceeded to walk as they conversed.

"Thinking about it, I assume that you were responsible for pulling out that Marine detachment before we had to do them any real harm? Or they did us harm," he added with a wry smile.

"Always looking over you, Striker, you know that," Brognola replied with humor. "Sure, it was me. But you can give Bear a lot of the credit. I pulled the trigger, but it was his probing that loaded the gun."

"Would I be right in thinking this had something to do with it?" Bolan pulled a two-day-old copy of the *Herald* from his pocket and indicated a paragraph concerning the sad death of a U.S. Senator in a road accident.

"There are a lot of accidents on our roads, Striker. I guess people need driver's ed more than you'd think. An unfortunate occurrence, and it creates a vacuum within a certain cabal. That, and the pressure brought on a colonel nearing retirement, may be in some manner connected."

"I see. Every action—"

"—has an equal and opposite reaction. Precisely."

"Our mission," Bolan said after a pause.

"What of it?" Brognola asked blandly.

"Was it worth it?"

Brognola took a deep breath. "Depends what you mean. From this country's point of view, the gentlemen you rescued will naturally be grateful to us. From their point of view, they're getting good care. It'll be a while before they recover from the psychological effects, but that will come."

"As long as Hassim didn't lose six men for nothing," Bolan mused.

"It's the price. He took the pay offered," Brognola shrugged.

"I know…" Bolan answered, hearing the echoes.

Six months later

GABRIEL AND HOENESS had spent the time since their kidnapping recovering in a clinic located in the Midwest. Their families had been flown to join them, and although they did not know it, the laboratories they had assembled in Switzerland were dismantled and shipped to a location out on the American West Coast, just south of the orange groves. Their treatment had been intensive but careful, and their shattered psyches pieced together again. Oddly, despite their initial reactions, it had been the older man who had responded better to treatment.

Finally they were free to leave—as far as the parking lot. There they were greeted by men in dark suits who ferried them to the nearest airstrip, where an unmarked jet was waiting to take them to the coast.

"Your families are waiting for you," the smooth suit on the plane told them. "But first, we need to show you where you will be working."

When the plane landed, they were taken in a limo with smoked glass to a compound located outside a small town. It seemed to be a small military post dealing with catering supplies. This was an impression belied by the elevator taking them down several hundred yards.

"General, it is time at last," the smooth suit said as the elevator discharged them. Gabriel and Hoeness looked at each other nervously.

"Gentlemen, you have nothing to fear," the general greeted them. "Follow me."

At the end of a corridor, they came out onto the gallery running around a floorspace that was peopled by two dozen scientists, all working at benches and with small-scale lab equipment.

Uli looked bemused. "But they're…"

A heavy-set, blue-suited figure joined them. His voice would have been familiar to the man he called Striker.

"Indeed, gentlemen. They are working on exactly the same thing as you. They have been for some time. This team has been assembled from all over the world. You may have believed you were working in isolation, but you were not. You may just be the final piece in the jigsaw that forms the picture of cold fusion."

The two scientists looked at him, puzzled.

"Welcome to the team. You're one of us, now, gentlemen, and you can trust us to look after you. After all, we pulled you out of the fire, right?"

The two scientists took in what was happening below

them and exchanged glances. The blue-suited man could read their expressions, and allowed himself a small smile.

Job done, thought Hal Brognola.

* * * * *